A friend in need . . .

This book to be returned on or before
the last date stamped below.

PASCAL, Francine

Hang out with the coolest kids around!

THE UNICORN CLUB

Created by Francine Pascal

Jessica and Elizabeth Wakefield are just two of the terrific members of The Unicorn Club you've met in *Sweet Valley Twins* books. Now get to know some of their friends even better!

A sensational *Sweet Valley* series.

SWEET VALLEY TWINS

Don't Talk to Brian

Written by
Jamie Suzanne

Created by
FRANCINE PASCAL

BANTAM BOOKS
NEW YORK · TORONTO · LONDON · SYDNEY · AUCKLAND

DON'T TALK TO BRIAN
A BANTAM BOOK : 0 553 50321 9

Originally published in USA by Bantam Books

First publication in Great Britain

PRINTING HISTORY
Bantam edition published 1996

Conceived by Francine Pascal

Produced by Daniel Weiss Associates, Inc,
33 West 17th Street, New York, NY 10011

Cover photo by Oliver Hunter

Bantam Books are published by Transworld Publishers Ltd,
61–63 Uxbridge Road, Ealing, London W5 5SA,
in Australia by Transworld Publishers (Australia) Pty Ltd,
15–25 Helles Avenue, Moorebank, NSW 2170,
and in New Zealand by Transworld Publishers (NZ) Ltd,
3 William Pickering Drive, Albany, Auckland.

Printed and bound in Great Britain by
Cox & Wyman Ltd, Reading, Berkshire.

To Emily Kathleen Jacobson

One

"Hey, Boyd, what happened to you?" Ken Matthews called out on Monday morning.

"Nice eye—when did you start wearing makeup?" Todd Wilkins asked.

Elizabeth Wakefield glanced up at Brian Boyd, who was walking into their homeroom with his typical swagger. Then she took a pencil out of her backpack and started arranging things on her desk. She didn't want to look at Brian for a second longer than she had to. She didn't care if he did have a black-and-blue eye.

Ever since Brian had moved to Sweet Valley, Elizabeth hadn't liked him. And that was even before he tried to get everyone to follow his every command in a classroom experiment they'd participated in a few weeks ago. Elizabeth had been the only one who resisted Brian's demands, and he'd practically bitten her head off for daring to disagree. She couldn't believe Ken and Todd even talked to Brian anymore after what a jerk he'd been to them.

Brian walked past Elizabeth to his desk just behind her. He had thick, short dark brown hair, and he was built like a football player, with broad shoulders. "Man, that was one of the worst fights I've ever been in," he boasted to Ken and Todd.

"Really. What happened?" Ken asked, sounding as if he didn't care much about the answer.

Brian slid into his chair and slammed his books down on his desk. "It was this guy who couldn't handle it when I kept beating him at Super Combat. I mean, I must have won about ten games in a row."

"Is that your favorite game or something?" Aaron Dallas asked. "You're always playing it."

"Favorite? No, I'm just great at it. What can I say—some of us are just born with natural talent," Brian bragged. "Just genius, I guess."

Elizabeth started scribbling angrily in the margins of her notebook. One of Brian's most offensive ideas was that some people were born better than others. He based all of his friendships on whether people were cool or not. Elizabeth shuddered. Attitudes like that made her sick. In her opinion it didn't matter whether people were cool or not; it mattered whether you could really count on your friends, especially when things got rough.

But Brian had been so spoiled his whole life, Elizabeth decided, that he'd probably never had to deal with anything difficult. He lived in a huge house in their neighborhood, and he always had tons of new clothes, the latest handheld video games, and about five mountain bikes.

"So did he challenge you to a fight, or what?" Todd asked.

"Oh yeah," Brian said. "He said something about how I was good at Super Combat, but I probably stunk at fighting in *real* life." Brian snickered. "Right. So I said, 'Dude, we'll see.' And we went out to the parking lot and just started swinging at each other."

"He must have gotten a great first punch," Ken commented. "That eye looks pretty bad."

"Yeah. He got a good first punch, but that's all," Brian said. "Then I whaled on him for, like, five minutes. He was hurting real bad when I left him. And this guy was at least a couple of years older than me and about a foot taller."

"Really?" Ken asked. Elizabeth thought he sounded a little frightened, almost as if he were afraid of Brian. She wasn't surprised; nearly all the kids at school were. "So you're good at fighting?"

"Yeah," Brian said. "I've got a mean right hook," he said. "Golden Gloves, here I come!"

Elizabeth grit her teeth and clenched her pencil more tightly. If there was one thing she hated, it was somebody who thought fighting was an OK thing to do. And there was Brian, *bragging* about how bad he had hurt another person.

Not that she believed him. Brian was probably exaggerating, the way he always did. Why did he have to move to Sweet Valley, anyway? She wished he'd stayed in Los Angeles, where he could bother everyone in his old school—and leave *her* alone.

"All right, everyone, listen up! I've got a fun project for you," Mr. Bowman announced later that morning.

Elizabeth smiled up at her English teacher. She loved her class with Mr. Bowman. English was her favorite subject, and she wanted to be a writer someday. Besides, Mr. Bowman was cool, always thinking of fun assignments.

"We're going to start a new topic of study. Now it may sound like it doesn't have much to do with English—"

"Are we studying Spanish?" Brian Boyd asked. A couple of students laughed.

"No," Mr. Bowman said slowly, with an irritated glance at Brian. "Actually, what we'll be studying for the next two weeks has less to do with language and more to do with people. As part of a new statewide focus, we'll be discussing parents and families."

"What do you mean?" Jessica Wakefield, Elizabeth's twin sister, asked. "We're going to sit around and talk about our families?"

"Sounds boring to me," her best friend, Lila Fowler, added under her breath.

Elizabeth had to smile at Lila's complaint. Lila usually loved nothing *better* than sitting around talking about people. Lila was one of the biggest gossips in school, and her best friend, Jessica, was a close second.

That was one of the many differences between Elizabeth and Jessica. Even though they looked identical, with their long blond hair and blue-green eyes, Jessica and Elizabeth were as different as two people could be.

Jessica liked hanging out with her friends in the Unicorn Club, gossiping, shopping, and plotting which boy to ask to the next dance. Elizabeth knew that Jessica didn't find Mr. Bowman's class as interesting as she did. In fact, even though Jessica was very smart, she didn't have that much interest in school right now, except as it related to her social life.

Elizabeth was more serious about her studying. She already knew she wanted to be a writer. She was one of the editors of the Sweet Valley Middle School newspaper, the *Sixers*, and she loved reading mystery novels. Not that she didn't enjoy hanging out with her friends, watching movies, and talking, too, but it wasn't a priority.

"To answer your question, Jessica, we won't necessarily be talking about anyone's family in particular," Mr. Bowman said. "But we will be studying the concept of good parenting and the makeup of the contemporary American family. And I sincerely hope it won't bore you too much, Lila." Mr. Bowman winked at Lila.

"We'll see," Lila replied, flipping her long hair over her shoulder.

"Now," Mr. Bowman continued, "we'll be doing different things in this unit, including discussions, role-playing skits, and writing essays for a contest. The winner will read his or her essay at a special reception for all of your parents."

"Gee, sounds thrilling," Brian scoffed. "Couldn't we just study Spanish instead?"

Elizabeth glared at him. Why did Brian have to ruin everything? She was looking forward to writing an essay about her family. *He probably thinks it's not cool enough,* she thought.

"Brian, this unit is very important, and whether you think it's thrilling or not, we'll be starting on it tomorrow," Mr. Bowman said, giving Brian a stern look. Then he returned to his desk at the front of the room. "All right, everyone, let's turn to our textbook and talk about the story I assigned for today."

"Save me," Elizabeth heard Brian mutter to Ken. "Is that the stupidest assignment you've ever heard of, or what?"

"Sounds OK to me," Ken said. "It sounds easy, actually."

"Yeah, I guess," Brian replied. "Considering it's a total waste of time, anyway."

Elizabeth flipped her textbook open to the short

story and tried to tune out Brian's voice. *He'd probably rather have another assignment where he could tell us all what to do,* she thought. He obviously didn't enjoy doing anything unless he was in charge.

Elizabeth thought about her own family for a second. It would be fun to write about them: Her mother was an interior designer, her father was a lawyer, and her older brother, Steven, was . . . well, a pain, most of the time.

But what was an essay without a little conflict?

"So guess what we're studying at school starting tomorrow!" Jessica said at dinner that night. She scooped potato salad onto her plate and passed the bowl to Steven.

"What? You're actually going to *study* something?" Steven asked, putting two huge spoonfuls of potato salad on his plate.

"Not that *you* would know anything about that," Elizabeth teased him.

Jessica looked at her sister and gave her a thumbs-up. As far as she was concerned, the more she and Elizabeth could gang up on their obnoxious fourteen-year-old brother, the better.

"Hey, just wait until you guys get to high school," Steven said. "You don't even know the meaning of the word exam."

"Like you do," Jessica retorted. "What did you get on your last chemistry test? A sixty-seven or a forty-seven?"

"Actually, it was a seventy-seven," Steven muttered. "But I got an A on my extra-credit project, so I have a B average."

"That's good," Mr. Wakefield said. "A little extra credit never hurt anyone."

"So what were you talking about, Jessica?" Mrs. Wakefield asked. "Something you're studying at school?"

"Well, Mr. Bowman announced that we're going to have this whole unit on parenting and families," Jessica said excitedly. "And it's going to be cool!"

"Since when are you so into English class?" Elizabeth asked, sounding skeptical.

Jessica sighed impatiently. She had to admit, writing English essays didn't exactly thrill her, but the more she thought about it, the more she liked the idea of Mr. Bowman's assignment. "I just think that this family thing Mr. Bowman was talking about sounds like fun."

"Family thing?" Mr. Wakefield asked curiously.

"We're going to write essays about our families," Jessica explained. "So everyone better be on their best behavior, because you never know what I might write about you."

"Yeah. Like I'm worried about what you write about me in your dumb essay," Steven scoffed.

"Actually, you should be," Jessica told him. "Because Mr. Bowman's going to pick an essay to be read at this huge reception at school for everyone's parents. And you wouldn't want to look bad in front of everyone, would you?" She gave Steven a superior look.

"I'm not exactly afraid of you winning," Steven replied. "Isn't Elizabeth in the same class?"

Jessica glared at him. "Yeah. So?"

"So, if there's an essay contest, Elizabeth will probably win. That means I only have to worry about being nice to *her*," Steven said with a shrug.

"Steven . . . ," Mr. Wakefield warned.

Jessica felt like throwing her roll at her brother. "Just because Elizabeth likes to write twenty-four hours a day, doesn't mean she's a better writer than me."

Steven laughed. "You're right, Jessica. I have seen you write something good. I think it was a shopping list!"

"Steven, that's not very nice," Mr. Wakefield said. "Jessica has just as good a chance of writing a winning essay as anyone."

"And if you put enough time into it, honey, I'm sure you'll do well," Mrs. Wakefield added.

Jessica brushed a crumb from the tablecloth onto the floor. It wasn't fair. She and Elizabeth both had to write about their families. That meant they had all the same material to use. And it was true that Elizabeth *was* a better writer. But did that mean she knew more about being part of a family? Did that mean she was a better daughter, or sister?

What do I care? Jessica thought. As far as Jessica was concerned, everyone ought to be worrying about living up to *her* expectations. She was the one who was going to be studying them. And if they didn't measure up, she would have even more to write about in her essay.

"Jessica, maybe we can work on our essays together," Elizabeth suggested.

"No thanks," Jessica replied, folding up her napkin. "I have my own ideas about what I want to write."

"Really? Like what?" Mr. Wakefield asked.

"Like . . . the fact that I've said a hundred times that I don't like ham, and we have it practically every other night," Jessica declared, poking at her uneaten slice with a fork. "In my opinion, being part of a family means getting your own way some of the time."

"More like all of the time," Steven teased her.

"Well, we'll be sure to keep that in mind," Mrs. Wakefield told Jessica. "No ham. I think we can handle that."

Good, Jessica thought. *Maybe I can use this whole family project to get even more things out of my parents.* Steven, of course, was a hopeless case. Not that she wanted anything from him, except for him to go away to college. And the sooner the better.

"And I don't like this ultra-skim milk either," Jessica said, holding up her half-empty glass.

"I'll get rid of it right away, Your Highness," Steven said, jumping to his feet. "You can put how polite I am in your essay."

"That's not exactly what I had in mind," Jessica

said. Her essay would be like a story on one of those investigating television shows: an exposé on her family. She could see it now . . . "The Wakefield Family—Exposed!"

One thing was for sure: Everyone had better start treating her with a lot more respect!

Two

◇

"About five or six pages should do it," Mr. Bowman told Elizabeth's English class on Tuesday morning. He was explaining their essay assignment, which was due in a little over a week. Elizabeth jotted a few notes to herself in her notebook. She already had some ideas. The essay would be easy for her to write, because she thought her parents did a great job.

"What? Six pages?" Jessica sputtered. "Why don't you just ask us to write a whole book?"

"Actually, I was considering it," Mr. Bowman said, straightening his tie. "But then I figured, you might want to save a project for high school."

"Yeah, like the prom," Lila said with a giggle. Then she cleared her throat. "Seriously, Mr. Bowman. I love my father and everything, but I don't know how I can write more than two pages about him. He's just not that interesting."

"Well, once you start thinking about it, I'm sure you won't have any trouble," Mr. Bowman said. "There's a lot about families and parenting that we all take for granted. Write about the obvious stuff, if you like."

Elizabeth raised her hand.

"Yes, Elizabeth?" Mr. Bowman asked.

"What kind of structure should we use?" she began. "I mean, is it supposed to sound like a study, or can we just write about how we feel?"

"You're welcome to use whatever form you like," Mr. Bowman replied. "Traditional essay, personal memoir, lyric verse . . ."

"Lyric what?" Lila said.

"I think he meant lyrics—you know, like to a song," Jessica told her.

Elizabeth had to suppress a laugh. "It's poetry," she corrected her twin.

Jessica frowned. "Whatever."

Mr. Bowman consulted his notebook. "Now, to give you a few ideas on what you might write about, let's discuss what we think being a parent is all about."

"Rules, mostly," Maria Slater said.

Elizabeth laughed. In a way, her friend was right, she decided; her parents were constantly making new rules for her and Jessica—and especially for Steven, now that he was in high school.

"Yes, rules definitely are involved," Mr. Bowman continued. "But also think about what the necessary elements of a good parent are. What are the basic requirements you kids have? What makes a family a family?" He went back to his desk. "To get you all started, I thought we could go around the room. Each person can tell the class what he or she thinks is important in a parent."

"Cash, and lots of it," Brian said loudly.

A few people in the room laughed nervously. Elizabeth frowned at Brian. Did he have to brag about how rich he was, on top of everything else?

"Brian, please wait your turn, all right?" Mr. Bowman said. "Amy, how about if you start?"

Elizabeth looked at Amy Sutton, one of her best friends, who was thinking it over. "I guess what's necessary for me is that my parents listen to me," she finally said.

"Ah. Communication." Mr. Bowman nodded. "Very important."

"Very important," Brian mimicked in a high, obnoxious voice.

Elizabeth glared at him over her shoulder just as he turned around and shot a spitball right into Amy's face.

"Quit it!" Amy cried.

"Brian!" Elizabeth exclaimed.

Mr. Bowman whirled around. "What's going on?"

Brian turned back around and shrugged. "I don't know."

"Brian hit me with a spitball," Amy complained.

"Brian . . . this is your final warning," Mr. Bowman said. "I want you to stop disrupting my class. Now who wants to go next?"

Elizabeth was too angry at Brian to answer. She was relieved when Maria raised her hand. "When you were talking about what makes a family a family, I started thinking of something my grandmother always says."

"Honey, I can't find my dentures!" Brian called out.

Elizabeth stared at him along with the rest of the class, openmouthed. She couldn't believe it. After Mr. Bowman had just warned him not to, he was already disrupting class again.

Mr. Bowman pushed his chair aside and walked over to Brian's desk. "OK, Brian, I think we've heard just about enough from you today. The rest of us are trying to have a serious discussion here, but if you don't want to participate, I'm sure Mr. Clark can find something for you to do." He pointed to the door. "I presume you know the way?"

Brian shoved his chair back and stood up. Then, grabbing his backpack off the floor, he headed out into the hallway.

What's Brian trying to prove, anyway? Elizabeth wondered. All he'd been doing lately was getting sent to the principal's office. *Must go along with his bully image,* she thought. For some reason, Brian was trying to prove to everyone how tough he was.

"Sorry about the interruption, Maria. What

were you saying?" Mr. Bowman asked once Brian was gone.

Maria looked a little flustered, but she managed a smile.

"My grandmother has this saying that she got from some book or movie," she said hesitantly. "I can't remember where."

"That's OK," Mr. Bowman said. "Tell us anyway."

"Well . . . it's something like this." Maria took a deep breath. "'Home is the place where they have to take you in.' Which means, basically, that no matter what you do or say, your family will still love you. And if they're a real family, they'll never abandon you, no matter what."

Mr. Bowman smiled and turned to write the saying on the blackboard.

"That's nice," Elizabeth whispered to her friend.

But Maria looked troubled. "Can you believe what Brian said? He's so rude!"

"Don't let him get to you," Elizabeth advised. "Believe me, ignoring Brian is the best thing you could do."

"No way. You are not going to ask Brian Boyd to that dance," Jessica said to Ellen Riteman, another member of the Unicorn Club, at lunch on Tuesday. They were sitting in the Unicorner, their "officially" reserved club spot in the school cafeteria.

"Why not?" Ellen asked.

"Because he's a jerk, that's why!" Jessica stared

at Ellen as she shook salt onto her french fries. "Haven't you noticed that he's the rudest person in this entire school?"

"So?" Ellen shrugged. "He's cute. Don't you remember how popular he was when he first moved here?"

Lila sighed impatiently. "That was before—well, you know, before it became obvious what an obnoxious bully he is."

Jessica nodded. She had to admit, it had taken her and the rest of the Unicorns a long time to realize what a jerk Brian was. But now that she did know, she wouldn't be caught dead with him at a dance.

"I can't imagine going to a dance with him," she told Ellen. "He'd interrupt you the whole night, make fun of your outfit, throw punch on you—no, definitely don't ask him."

"OK, OK! It was just an idea," Ellen said.

"A bad idea," Janet Howell said.

Jessica was glad Janet agreed. People usually listened to Janet. She was an eighth-grader and the president of the Unicorn Club. She also happened to be Lila's cousin and was almost as wealthy.

"Brian's probably going to get kicked out of school before the dance anyway," Jessica boldly predicted. "Ellen, you'd better focus on someone a little nicer. Like . . . anyone else, actually." She dipped a fry in ketchup and popped it into her mouth.

"Speaking of the dance . . ." Lila looked expectantly at Jessica. "What are you going to wear?"

Jessica tapped a french fry against her plate and tried to look casual. She'd been dreading this question ever since the dance was announced. "I don't know," she said. *The same thing I wore to the last dance? A tutu? Maybe a barrel?*

"Well, I've got the coolest new dress—it's one of those that has tiny straps and then you wear a little white T-shirt underneath," Lila said.

"Oh, I love those," Ellen gushed. "My mom got me a new dress for this big family party last week, so I'll probably wear that. It's this really deep blue, with little gold-and-white flowers."

"Sounds nice," Jessica mumbled, sinking lower in her seat. The truth was, she didn't have any idea what she would wear to the dance. But she knew that whatever it was, it wasn't at home in her closet right now. It was at a department store, hanging on a rack, with her name on it. The only problem was, she couldn't possibly buy it. She had no allowance left, and her savings account was as empty as it could be without being permanently closed by the bank.

"I have the coolest black-and-white dress—I got it when I was visiting my cousin in San Francisco a couple of weeks ago," Janet announced. She turned to Jessica. "So what are you wearing?"

"Well . . . I definitely need something new. Something everyone hasn't seen before and no one else has," Jessica said. *And something absolutely free.*

"Do you want to hit the mall this afternoon?" Lila asked.

Jessica hesitated, pushing an empty granola bar wrapper around on the table. "Sure," she said. "There's just one slight problem. I don't—"

"Have any money," Lila completed the sentence for her. "Well, what else is new?" She shrugged.

"Nothing," Jessica sighed. "But I'm considering asking my parents for an advance on my next allowance. Maybe if I explain how important a new dress is, they'll advance me the money," she said as hopefully as possible.

Janet raised an eyebrow. "Are you kidding? No offense, Jessica, but your parents don't exactly understand the importance of clothes."

"Yeah, and don't you already owe them, like, three months' allowance for the dress you wore to the last big dance?" Ellen reminded her.

Jessica frowned. She had kind of forgotten about that. Getting a dress out of her parents was going to be even tougher than she thought. She strummed her fingers on the table, when suddenly she had an idea. "I know!" she exclaimed, dropping the french fry from her hand. "I have the perfect solution."

"Apply for your own credit card?" Lila scoffed.

"I'll ask my parents to *raise* my allowance," Jessica said triumphantly. It was genius. Absolute genius. "It's been forever since it went up," she went on excitedly. "And the raise will be enough to cover what I owe from before, so then they can give me an advance."

Janet looked skeptical. "You really think your parents are going to raise your allowance that much?"

Jessica shrugged. "Why not? I'm *worth* it, aren't I, darling?" She flipped her hair over her shoulder dramatically.

"If you say so," Lila teased. "We'll see."

Finally, I'm out of this stupid place. Brian Boyd pushed open the front door of Sweet Valley Middle School and walked out into the late afternoon sunshine. He hurried over to the bicycle rack to unlock his mountain bike. Then he remembered he wasn't in any rush to get home. Even though he was glad to be out of his all-afternoon detention—supervised personally by Mr. Clark—he wasn't anxious to see his parents. Maybe a few months ago he would have been, but not now. Now everything was different.

Brian got onto his bike and started riding slowly toward his house. He took the long way, through the park, doing a couple of circles on the bike path. Mr. Clark had phoned his mother from school, and Brian knew she would be furious. And his father . . . Brian didn't even want to think about how his father would react to the news that he'd gotten in trouble again.

On the other hand, if he got home too late, they'd probably be even more upset with him.

Either way, it's not going to be pleasant. Brian picked up the pace and arrived at his front door about ten minutes later. He put his bike in the garage and walked into the house.

"Brian! Is that you?" his mother called from the kitchen.

Brian stopped, his hand on the stair banister. He'd been hoping he could disappear to his room before she heard him. "Hi, Mom," he said. "I'm going to start my homework—"

"Not so fast! Mr. Clark called this afternoon!" Mrs. Boyd yelled. "He said you were in trouble again."

Brian cringed. From the way his mother was talking, he could tell that she had been drinking. Whenever she drank too much alcohol, she started talking in this weird, harsh way, slurring her *s*'s and practically shouting at him.

"Brian, you're messing up!" she went on. "What the heck is wrong with you?" his mother demanded.

"I'm sorry, Mom," Brian called to her. He didn't want to go into the kitchen. If he could just make it to his room and put on some loud music, everything would be OK. "I'm going to study now."

"You'd better!" she replied harshly. "Because I'm telling you right now, your father is not going to like this one bit! And when he gets home, you'd better have a good explanation!"

Brian took the steps two at a time. Once he was in his room, he closed the door and leaned against it, panting and out of breath. His mother's words kept echoing in his head: *"When your father gets home . . ."*

He used to love waiting for his father to get home. Now he dreaded it. They used to play one-on-one at the basketball hoop over the garage, or hang out on the porch just talking about stuff. That seemed like such a long time ago, he could barely remember how it felt. It was almost as if it had happened to someone else. Now . . . they never played or talked. And now Brian was scared to death of seeing his father.

He heard his father's car pull into the driveway and the engine shut off. Brian turned the bolt lock on his bedroom door. *Please, Dad*, he thought. *Please be in a good mood tonight.*

Please don't hit me.

Three

Tuesday night, Elizabeth was staring at a diagram in her science textbook, trying to study for a quiz the next morning. But she couldn't concentrate. There was the strangest noise coming through her window.

The alley that ran behind the Wakefield house was home to a few stray cats, which Jessica was always feeding. And it wasn't unusual to hear the cats meowing or having the occasional fight. But for some reason, tonight it sounded like one of them was crying. *That's ridiculous*, Elizabeth told herself. *Cats don't cry.* Or at least not the same way people do.

She pushed her chair back from her desk and peered out her bedroom window, but she couldn't make out anything in the alley. She went downstairs, out the back door, and crossed the patio by the pool. There was a tall wooden fence separating the Wakefields' yard from the alley. Elizabeth carefully began to climb it, putting her foot on a toehold halfway up.

When she peered over the top of the fence, Elizabeth saw a boy sitting in the alley, on top of a stack of old magazines waiting to be recycled. The boy's head was buried in his hands, and he was sobbing. Elizabeth stared at his figure, his dark hair, and his black leather high-top sneakers. She couldn't believe her eyes. It was Brian Boyd!

Elizabeth's foot slipped off the ledge, and she grabbed the top of the fence with her hands. She hung by the tips of her fingers for a second until she could get another grip with her shoes.

The fence squeaked loudly, and Brian looked up at Elizabeth with surprise. He hastily brushed the tears off his face and stood up. "What are you doing here?" he asked.

"I—I live here," Elizabeth stammered, nodding to the house behind her. She felt nervous, as if she'd been caught spying—which, she guessed, she basically had been. "Is . . . is everything OK?" she asked.

Brian glared at her. "Get lost!" he barked.

Elizabeth looked at him for another second. His face seemed swollen, and she felt a pang of concern. What if Brian was really hurt? After all, he'd been crying loudly enough for her to hear him from inside her house. "Brian, are you sure you're OK? I mean, can I help you or—"

"Can't you hear? I said get lost!" Brian shouted.

Elizabeth climbed down the fence into her yard, trembling. She hated being yelled at, especially by a bully like Brian. All she'd wanted was to see if he was all right—she hated to see anyone upset. But if he was going to react that way, she didn't care how he felt.

He probably got hurt in another fight, and that's why he was crying, Elizabeth told herself. With a quick glance over her shoulder, she crossed the patio and went back into the house, closing the door firmly behind her. If Brian wanted to be a bully and start fights, that was his problem. Then he deserved whatever happened to him.

"Mom, that's such a nice suit!" Jessica greeted her mother Wednesday morning at breakfast. "And that silk blouse you're wearing underneath." She sat down at the kitchen table and smiled at her mother. "It's gorgeous!"

Mrs. Wakefield smiled. "Well, thank you." She poured milk into her bowl of cereal.

"So, is the suit new?" Jessica asked. She reached for a glass and poured herself some orange juice.

"Yes, it is. I picked it up during the one-day sale at Woodman's last week." Jessica's mother gave her a questioning look. "Why?"

"Oh, no reason." Jessica shrugged. "It's just nice,

that's all." *Everything's going according to plan.*

"She wants something," Steven informed his mother, rubbing his eyes as he walked into the kitchen. "Trust me, Mom, it's the only time she's nice."

"That's not true!" Jessica objected. "I'm nice all the time, unlike *some* people I know." She frowned at Steven. Why did he have to interrupt just when she was making progress? Couldn't Steven have stayed in bed just ten minutes longer? Some people had no consideration.

She looked at Elizabeth across the table, expecting her sister to come to her defense. But Elizabeth was staring into space as she chewed a piece of toast. She looked exhausted. Her father was sitting beside her, studying that morning's *Sweet Valley Tribune.*

"Late night, Elizabeth?" Jessica asked. "Don't tell me you stayed up writing your essay."

"Essay?" Elizabeth repeated vaguely. "Oh, that. No."

Jessica had never seen her twin look so out of it. *Oh, well. That's not my problem. Convincing Mom and Dad to give me more money is.* She turned back to her mother and cleared her throat. "So *anyway*, Mom," she began in a low voice. "I was wondering about something."

"Dad, can I have the sports section?" Steven asked. The newspaper rustled in front of Jessica's face as Mr. Wakefield handed it to Steven. Jessica glared at her brother.

"What is it?" Mrs. Wakefield asked.

"Well, it's just that . . . you know about inflation, right?" Jessica asked, turning back to her mother and smiling.

"Boy, do I," her mother said, nodding.

"And you know how things get more expensive all the time and how hard it is to live on a fixed income," Jessica said.

"Are you writing a paper about Social Security now?" Mr. Wakefield asked, looking up from the paper.

"No," Jessica said slowly. "I'm still working on my parenting essay. You know, the one where I have to evaluate whether you guys are good parents and siblings and all that?" She looked around the table meaningfully.

"And how is that going?" Mr. Wakefield asked.

"Oh, fine," Jessica said casually. "At least . . . so *far*. But the thing is, Mom and Dad, I want to ask you about something for me. I mean, for me and Elizabeth, I guess."

"Is this about getting your ears pierced again?" her mother said.

"No, nothing like that," Jessica said. "It's about . . . a raise. In our allowance."

Steven laughed. "A raise? That's ridiculous."

"It is not!" Jessica protested.

"If anyone around here gets a raise, it should be *me*," Steven continued.

"*You?*" Jessica asked. "Why on earth would you need a raise?"

"Because I have way more expenses than you do." Steven sat up straighter in his chair. "I mean, I *am* fourteen."

"Yeah—going on eight!" Jessica muttered.

"I don't want either one of you getting your hopes up," Mrs. Wakefield said. "I'm not sure we can afford to give anyone a raise in their allowance right now."

"But, Mom," Jessica complained. "You guys have been giving us the same amount for, like, a decade. Costs have gone way up. I can't even afford new lip balm, never mind a new dress for the dance party that's coming up—"

"Ah ha!" Mr. Wakefield cried. "Now we're getting somewhere." He grinned at Jessica. "This cost-of-living raise wouldn't have anything to do with a dance, would it?"

"It's just a coincidence," Jessica said quickly. "There happens to be this dance, and I do need a new dress, but that's not the point."

"It isn't?" Mrs. Wakefield asked.

"No, it isn't," Jessica insisted. "The point is that Elizabeth and I need lots of things, all the time, and the allowance you've been giving us just won't cover it all. And parents ought to listen to their children when their needs aren't being met—that's what Mr. Bowman said. And we need more money."

"Is that true, Elizabeth?" her father asked. "Do you really need more money?"

"Huh?" Elizabeth turned and looked at everyone.

"Tell them, Elizabeth. We need a raise in our allowance," Jessica said. She looked at her sister's glazed expression. *Of all the times for Elizabeth to turn into a space cadet!* "I mean, it's absolutely necessary, right?" she asked her.

Elizabeth stared at her without saying a word.

Come on, Elizabeth, Jessica thought, concentrating on her twin. *Wake up and help me here.*

"Let me try something," Steven said, turning in his chair. "Elizabeth, do you have five dollars I could borrow until Friday?"

"Sure," Elizabeth said, reaching into her pocket and pulling out a few bills.

Jessica glared at her brother. "Look, the only reason you need a loan is because you ran out of money just like me, which only proves my point! And Elizabeth only has money left over because she never buys anything and she doesn't care if she wears the same dress to every single dance!"

Elizabeth turned to her, a hurt expression on her face. "What did you just say?"

"It's not my fault nobody else here cares what they look like," Jessica complained.

"I care—I just think there are more important things in life than clothes," Elizabeth argued.

"Obviously!" Jessica cried, throwing up her hands.

"OK, Jessica, settle down," Mr. Wakefield interrupted. "There's no need to insult your sister. We've listened to your request, and we'll take it into consideration, but for right now, your allowance will remain the same. And as I recall, you still owe us three months' worth for the last advance we gave you."

Steven grinned at Jessica. "Want to borrow one of my suits for the dance? I hear the menswear look is in this year."

Jessica drummed her fingernails against the table. The way things were going, nobody was going to look very good in her parenting and family essay. Certainly not her brother. Definitely not her parents. Even Elizabeth was on shaky ground. Of course she cared about more than just clothes. It was just that at this particular *moment*, clothes happened to be the most important thing. Clothes, and money to buy them with. Only nobody in her family could possibly understand that. And because of that, nobody in her family would come out sounding very good in her essay for Mr. Bowman.

And now, because Elizabeth didn't take her side, Jessica wasn't going to look good for the dance. When your own twin sister wouldn't back you up on something, what did that say about family?

Jessica pulled a piece of scrap paper and a pen out of the kitchen drawer. IMPORTANT IN A FAMILY: SUPPORTING EACH OTHER, she wrote. ESPECIALLY WHEN SOMEBODY REALLY REALLY NEEDS SOMETHING.

Four

"So, has everyone been working on their essays?"
Mr. Bowman asked at the beginning of English
class on Thursday morning.

"Yeah, right," Elizabeth heard Brian Boyd mutter behind her.

Sure, Brian didn't have time to work on his essay,
she thought. He was too busy picking fights.
Elizabeth had been concerned when she'd caught
Brian crying two nights before, but that didn't
mean she liked him. She couldn't connect the
image of Brian crying to the image of him sitting in
class making dumb remarks . . . or yelling at her to
leave him alone.

"Well, I'm working on *my* essay," Jessica announced loudly. "In fact, I've been taking notes
constantly."

Elizabeth turned and stared at her sister. She hadn't even started thinking about her essay yet—and Jessica was already writing hers? Had somebody switched their brains overnight?

"That's great," Mr. Bowman said. "Any questions so far?"

"Yeah. How do we get out of doing it?" Brian whispered to Todd.

Elizabeth shook her head. Typical. Brian never actually wanted to do anything—except make other people miserable.

"OK then. Let me explain what we'll be up to this morning," Mr. Bowman said. "I thought we'd perform a couple of skits. You've all heard of role playing, right?"

Elizabeth nodded.

"Sure," Maria said.

"I've picked a few situations for which I'm curious to see how you all think a parent would act and how a child might act. Now I've never done this before, so bear with me." Mr. Bowman picked some index cards off the top of his desk and shuffled through them. "OK, who'd like to volunteer?"

Elizabeth shifted uneasily in her seat. Usually she was one of the first to volunteer for in-class projects, but she just didn't feel like acting in front of everyone. Plays weren't her thing—they were more Jessica's speed. Apparently no one else felt like volunteering either. Everyone sat quietly in their seats.

"All right, since you're all so eager, how about . . . Maria, Elizabeth . . . and Brian," Mr. Bowman said.

"Oh, great," Maria muttered as she and Elizabeth stood up. "We get to work with the creep of the year."

"Do I have to?" Brian said. "I don't like acting. I mean, I have this stage-fright thing and—"

"Brian, you're the least shy person I know," Mr. Bowman said. The class laughed. "Now just please come up here and we'll get started."

Elizabeth walked to the front of the room and waited while Mr. Bowman set up a few chairs for them. She glanced at Brian. His eye was still a little black and blue, and he had a large yellow-green bruise on his forearm. When he saw her looking at it, he pulled down the sleeves of his shirt and buttoned them at the wrist.

She wondered why he kept getting into fights if he was obviously losing them so badly. She remembered him yelling at her the night before when she was only trying to be nice. She shook her head, trying to make the memory disappear. Brian wasn't worth worrying about if he was going to act like that. "So what should we do?" she asked Mr. Bowman. She wanted to get the whole thing over with as soon as possible.

"Maria and Brian will play the mother and father," Mr. Bowman said. "Elizabeth, you'll be the child."

"Woo-ooh!" Charlie Cashman whistled. "Maria and Brian!"

"Shut up." Maria rolled her eyes.

"Yeah, grow up," Brian added. "We're playing *roles*, OK?"

"If everyone could please settle down, we'll begin," Mr. Bowman said, sounding slightly amused. "Here's the situation, guys. Elizabeth, you have a curfew. You're supposed to be home every night by ... let's say ... eight. But you have a party you want to go to, and you're not taking no for an answer."

"Oh, I get it," Elizabeth said without thinking. "All I have to do is act like Jessica!"

"What?" Jessica sat up in her seat. "What are you saying?"

Elizabeth giggled, and the rest of the class cracked up laughing.

Mr. Bowman cleared his throat. "Resemblance to any persons living or dead is purely coincidental."

"I certainly hope so," Jessica declared in a snooty tone. Everyone laughed some more.

"So," Mr. Bowman went on, "you sneak out of your room, go to the party ... and when you come home—surprise! Your parents are waiting for you. How would you react? Remember, Brian and Maria, you're parents trying to do the right thing, and Elizabeth, you're a kid who's sick of all the rules," Mr. Bowman instructed the three of them. "Now, Elizabeth, make your entrance."

Elizabeth went out into the hall for a second, then walked through the door in a crouched position, as if she were sneaking into a house.

"Elizabeth!" Maria cried. "Where on earth have you been?"

Elizabeth looked sheepishly at Maria. "Sorry, Mom."

"Sorry isn't good enough," Maria said. "It's almost eleven o'clock!"

Brian shifted from one foot to the other and stared up at the ceiling as if he was bored.

"Well, what do you have to say for yourself?" Maria asked.

Elizabeth shrugged. "I don't know. Look . . . I know I wasn't supposed to go, but everyone was going to be there, and I just couldn't miss the biggest party of the year over some dumb curfew." Elizabeth smiled to herself. She was better at this than she thought! She'd learned a lot from Jessica over the years.

"So you decided to sneak out and worry us half to death?" Maria asked. She turned to Brian, who was now staring at the floor. "Say something," she urged. "She's your daughter, too."

Brian looked at Elizabeth, an uneasy expression on his face. "So," he finally said. "Was it a good party?"

The class erupted in laughter. Maria frowned at him. Elizabeth was angry, too. Brian was supposed to be helping them, not cracking jokes.

"That's not the point," Maria said sternly. "The point is, she disobeyed our rules."

"Yeah, well." Brian shrugged. "Rules are meant to be broken, right?"

Mr. Bowman raised his hand. "May I make a comment? Brian, I wonder if you could get into the role a bit more. I know it's hard, but try to imagine that for the moment you're a parent. How would you feel?"

"How should *I* know?" Brian protested, throwing up his hands.

"Well, just try, Brian," Mr. Bowman urged. "I mean, wouldn't you be upset in this situation? Wouldn't you have worried about Elizabeth? I mean, if you were the father and your daughter came home late—"

"I *get* it," Brian interrupted, sounding impatient. "I'm not stupid. I just think it's a dumb *game*, OK?"

Mr. Bowman frowned at Brian. "Everyone's entitled to his opinion. But you will be graded on this."

Brian shook his head and stared at the floor, glowering.

Elizabeth decided to ignore him. She looked at Maria. "So, am I grounded?"

"Yeah," Brian suddenly piped up. "For life."

On her way home from school that afternoon, Elizabeth saw a police car pass her, going incredibly fast. She jammed on the brakes of her bike. She stopped so abruptly that her tires screeched to a halt. The police car was turning into the Boyds' driveway!

She slid off the bike seat and looked down Brian's driveway. Two other cars were parked up close to the house—official-looking cars, with the California state seal on the doors and license plates.

Elizabeth gasped. What was going on? It looked like a major crime scene! Maybe there had been an accident . . . maybe one of Brian's parents was hurt. Or maybe Brian was in trouble. Real trouble. With the police. Things seemed pretty serious.

She'd sensed that something was wrong with him over the past week, but she'd thought it was only because his rebellious attitude got him into trouble. But she'd never dreamed that the police would be involved. What had Brian done now?

She paused at the end of the driveway for a minute, hoping she might see something to let her know everything was all right. But nobody came out of the house. Since the police car's lights weren't flashing and there was no ambulance in sight, Elizabeth decided it must not be an emergency, though it did look strange. Brian had probably just done something stupid, like getting into another fight at the mall. Typical.

"Care for an appetizer, madame?" Jessica held a bowl of popcorn out to Elizabeth when she got home. "Mom says dinner won't be for another hour, at least. She's finishing up some project at the office."

Elizabeth took a handful of popcorn and slowly chewed a kernel. "You're not going to believe this," she said. "I went by the Boyds' house, and there was a police car there, and a couple of other official state cars—"

"You're kidding!" Jessica exclaimed. "Police cars? What happened?"

"I don't know." Elizabeth sighed. "Maybe Brian got into a fight—"

"Like he always does," Jessica commented.

"Right. But I hope he's not . . . you know . . . in trouble or anything," Elizabeth said.

"Since when do you care about Brian Boyd?" Jessica asked, looking incredulous.

"Oh, I don't really *care* about him," Elizabeth said. She wasn't about to tell Jessica what she'd overheard in the alley the other night. It was too personal, even to share with her twin. "It just seems kind of odd, that's all."

Jessica snapped her fingers. "You know what I bet it was? The Boyds are rich, right? I mean, they have that huge house, and Brian's always bragging about all the stuff he has—I bet they were robbed!"

Elizabeth considered her sister's suggestion. "Maybe."

"Ha. And you think *you* should be a mystery writer," Jessica scoffed. "Wow, I hope that thief doesn't come here. Wouldn't it be horrible to have all our stuff stolen?"

"Well, better than some things that could happen," Elizabeth said. She thought of the way Brian had been sobbing in the alley, as if he were the most miserable and lonely person in the entire world.

"Like what? What are you talking about?" Jessica tossed a piece of popcorn into her mouth and stared at Elizabeth.

Elizabeth shook her head. "Never mind. You're probably right about the break-in anyway." At least she *hoped* that Jessica was right.

"So you never told me—what did your parents say?" Lila asked when Jessica answered the phone Thursday night.

"About what?" Jessica replied.

"The raise," Lila said. "Are you going to get it?"

Jessica frowned. "Oh. That. Not exactly."

"In other words, no" Lila said.

"Well . . . they're taking it into consideration," Jessica said, trying to sound hopeful.

"Like I said—no," Lila repeated flatly. "No offense, Jessica. Your parents are really nice and sweet and everything, but they have no concept of finances."

Jessica sighed. "Tell me about it."

"I mean, my father might be gone a lot on business trips, but at least when I ask for something, I get it," Lila continued in a haughty tone.

Jessica bristled. She and Lila had been best friends for years, but Lila still never missed a chance to point out just how rich she was. As if Jessica could possibly forget that Lila had more money than she could even imagine. "Well . . . your dad buys you things, but that doesn't mean he's the perfect parent," she told Lila. "Parenting means being there, communicating—"

"Give me a break," Lila said. "I feel like I'm on a talk show."

"Sorry," Jessica said. "It's just that I've been thinking about this stuff a lot since I've been working on my essay and everything."

Lila gasped. "Jessica, you're really starting to scare me! The essay's not due till next week, and you're already working on it? Are you feeling OK?"

"Please. I can be as dedicated to homework as anyone," Jessica replied. "It just has to be the right topic, that's all." She had to admit that it was a *bit* unusual for her to work so far ahead of schedule, but Lila didn't have to rub it in.

"And what about this topic is so exciting?" Lila asked. "Because if you ask me, it's a major snooze."

"Well, I'm using the essay to rate my family," Jessica told Lila. "I'm recording all their behavior."

"And how's everyone doing?" Lila asked.

"Not so hot," Jessica replied. "Actually, I haven't found one good thing to say yet. Boy are they going to be embarrassed when I read my essay in front of all the other parents."

Lila sighed. "Jessica. You're not planning to *win* this thing, are you?"

Jessica frowned. Why did Lila have to make it sound as if there was no way Jessica could write a winning essay?

"You never know," she told Lila. "I think

my essay's going to be very eye-opening."

"If you say so—," Lila began. "Oh, my gosh. Will you look at my feet? I have to go put on a fresh coat of toenail polish *immediately*."

"OK. Hey, did you know the police were at Brian Boyd's house this afternoon?" Jessica asked.

"Why? What happened?" Lila asked excitedly.

"I'm not sure, but I think their house was broken into," Jessica said. "You and your dad better be careful—there might be a big-time thief looking for mansions to steal from." Since she'd had such a good hunch, she figured the least she could do was share it with her friends. Her rich friends, anyway.

"Excuse me, but that's why we have security guards," Lila said.

"Sorry!" Jessica said, laughing. "Excuse *me*!"

"So, do you want to come over this weekend? I'll let you look through my closet for something to wear to the dance," Lila offered. "I have some really cute stuff from last year that I never wore."

Jessica grit her teeth. She didn't really want to wear one of Lila's last-year's-style-hand-me-downs to the dance. If her parents would only raise her allowance, she wouldn't have to borrow things from other people. It was humiliating. Didn't they know they were ruining her self-esteem? And it was the parents' job, according to the handout Mr. Bowman had given them, to boost their kids' self-esteem. Not destroy it!

Still, she didn't actually want to wear anything

in her own closet. "Sure, that sounds OK," she told Lila. If she was going to wear hand-me-downs, at least they'd be designer ones.

"Psst. Elizabeth," Maria whispered to her friend on Friday morning.

Elizabeth turned to look at her while Mr. Bowman was busy taking attendance. "What's up? Do you need something?"

Maria nodded. "I forgot my notebook. Can I borrow some paper?"

Elizabeth tore a few sheets out of her notebook and handed them to Maria. "Here you go."

"Thanks," Maria said.

"Hmm. We seem to be missing a few people this morning—they must be taking long weekends!" Mr. Bowman joked as he jotted down a few things in his attendance record.

Elizabeth glanced over her shoulder at the empty chair in back of her. Brian Boyd was one of the people missing. She hadn't seen him around at school that day, in homeroom or anywhere else, so it wasn't as if he was just ditching Mr. Bowman's class. He probably wasn't feeling well, she decided. A lot of people had gotten the flu lately.

Then she remembered the police cars at his house the afternoon before. Was there some kind of connection between Brian not being at school today . . . and the police cars? And what about the night she'd caught him in the alley behind her house, sobbing as if his world was falling apart?

But knowing Brian, he was probably just playing hooky so he could hang out at home and play video games. Then he'd come to school Monday, bragging about how many games he won.

Elizabeth decided to relax. Whatever the reason for his absence from school, English class was a much calmer place without him.

Five

"And what are your plans for this gorgeous Saturday?" Mrs. Wakefield asked Elizabeth as she sat down at the kitchen table the next morning.

Elizabeth rubbed her eyes. "First, I want to wake up!" She laughed. "Second, I think I'll read the paper and hang out for a while before I meet Amy and Maria. We're going on a bike ride."

"That sounds nice," her mother said. "Well, I'm going to do a little work on the garden—come outside and visit me after breakfast, OK?"

Elizabeth nodded, spreading out the local section of the newspaper on the table in front of her. She always liked reading the neighborhood and human-interest stories. She read "Cat Saved By Firefighters in Two-Alarm Blaze" and "Local Merchants Unite to Save Free Parking" before she spotted an article with a less cheerful headline: "State Officials Remove Child From Home; Investigated Abuse." Elizabeth had been about to take a sip of orange juice, but she set her glass back on the table, her stomach churning nervously. She hated to read about things like that; she hated to know things like that happened. And she especially couldn't understand how parents could be mean to their children. It just wasn't *fair*.

She started to read the article. "'After responding to an abusive situation at the house for the third time in the past six months, Sweet Valley Police called in Child Protective Services, who arranged to put the twelve-year-old child in foster care until a thorough investigation can take place.'"

Twelve years old, Elizabeth thought, feeling sick to her stomach. *Just like me.*

"'While no formal charges have been filed, the state feels there is enough evidence to suggest that the child's welfare is in danger. Measures like this are often taken by the state in order to ensure children's safety. The parents will appear at a hearing before a judge next week to face charges of child abuse and to determine whether the child will be permanently removed from his home.'"

Elizabeth stared out the window, trying to imagine how horrible that situation would be. The police coming to your house and taking you away, all because your parents hurt you and—

That was when it hit her. A twelve-year-old . . . the

police . . . those state cars she'd seen . . . somebody who was hurt, possibly bruised . . . "Oh, no," she said out loud. "It's *Brian!*"

"What's Brian?" Jessica asked as she slid into a chair next to Elizabeth.

Elizabeth glanced over at her sister, completely terrified by what she'd just thought. She felt like her heart was in her throat.

"Elizabeth, is it about Brian Boyd?" Jessica asked. Elizabeth nodded. "Oh, my gosh, your face is, like, completely pale. Are you OK?"

Elizabeth slowly shook her head. "No. I mean, yes. I'm OK." *Brian's not.*

"Well, what's the big deal about Brian?" Jessica demanded.

"N-nothing," Elizabeth stammered. Brian probably wouldn't want everyone to know what was happening to him. Besides, she didn't know for *sure* that the article was about Brian.

"So why did you just say, 'Oh, no, it's Brian'?" Jessica demanded.

"I . . ." Elizabeth glanced down at the newspaper. She didn't know what to say. Part of her was dying to share her suspicions with her twin, but part of her felt she ought to keep them to herself.

"He's in the paper, isn't he?" Jessica grabbed the newspaper off the table and scanned the front page of the section. "But there's nothing here about an obnoxious kid from Sweet Valley Middle School. Unless . . . wait a second. You're not talking about *this*, are you?" She pointed to the article about investigated abuse.

Elizabeth grabbed the paper from her sister. "No," she said. "I mean, it's a terrible thing to happen . . . to anyone."

"It sure is," Jessica agreed. "But—is that 'someone' Brian?"

Elizabeth shrugged. "I don't know."

"Come on, Elizabeth. If it isn't Brian, then what were you talking about when you said his name?" Jessica asked.

Elizabeth hated trying to keep secrets from Jessica—it was nearly impossible. But was it right to share Brian's secret—when she didn't even know if it was true?

"Elizabeth!" Jessica cried, scooting her chair closer to her. "Come on. This is important!"

"It's just a . . . suspicion," she finally confessed. "I don't know for sure. So don't say anything to anyone, OK? There are some things that kind of add up, which made me think of Brian."

"Like what?" Jessica asked. Then she slapped her palm against the table. "Oh, my gosh! The police cars the other night. And how Brian kept saying he got into those fights and how he has those bruises and—Elizabeth, you're right! This is terrible! Even if Brian's a creep."

Elizabeth let out her breath. As much as she wanted to be fair to Brian, it was such a relief to talk to her sister. "Jessica, maybe that's *why* he's so mean all the time," she suggested slowly. "I mean . . . what if things are really rotten at his house and that's why he's such a jerk to everyone else . . ."

"Wow," Jessica said slowly, putting down the newspaper. "This is amazing. I thought this stuff only happened in big cities or on TV."

"Yeah," Elizabeth said with a sigh. "I did, too." A picture of Brian's black-and-blue eye flashed through her mind. "Jessica, please don't tell anyone—promise me you won't. We don't even know it's Brian for sure. And if it *is* him, I know he wouldn't want anyone to find out."

"Oh, I won't tell anyone," Jessica said. "I don't even want to think about it, never mind *talk* about it. You can trust me."

"It's too bad you didn't get the raise in your allowance. That dress looked cute on you," Janet said breezily as Lila, Jessica, and she walked into Casey's ice cream parlor Saturday afternoon. They had just finished trying on clothes at Valley Fashions.

"I guess this means I'll be buying you a cone again?" Lila asked.

"No," Jessica said. "I don't want a cone. I'm having a sundae, and I can pay for it myself, thank you very much." She fingered the collection of dimes and nickels she had found under the rugs in her room that morning. *I can pay for it as long as nothing fell out of my pocket, that is.*

"Not feeling a little sensitive today, are we?"

Janet teased, sliding into a booth by some Sweet Valley High students.

Lila put her purse over the back of a chair and sat down. "Jessica, *we* don't care how much money you have—"

"Or don't have," Janet added with a giggle.

"Right," Lila said. "I mean, how long have we been friends already, and you've always been broke."

"It's not my fault!" Jessica insisted. "My parents just happen to be stuck in the eighties when it comes to money." *Or was it the seventies?*

"Well, don't worry about it," Janet said. "I'm sure they'll get a clue eventually."

"Yeah," Jessica said. "I hope so."

Joe Carrey, one of their favorite waiters at Casey's, came to their table. Jessica smiled at him. "Hi, Joe," she said.

"Greetings, girls," Joe said. "Taking a break from studying?"

"More like a break from shopping," Jessica confessed.

Joe nodded. "Well, I was trying to give you the benefit of the doubt, but it was kind of hard, considering all the shopping bags you have," he said. The girls laughed. "So what'll it be?" he asked.

Jessica did some quick calculations while Lila and Janet placed their orders. *Let's see . . . two twenty-five plus tax . . .*

"And for you, Jessica?" Joe asked.

"I'll have a hot-fudge sundae," she said confidently.

But the numbers she'd been computing in her head suddenly clicked into a higher total than she'd imagined. "Uh . . . a small sundae, that is," she added, feeling embarrassed. "I guess I'm not as hungry as I thought."

Janet gave Lila a knowing look, and they both giggled.

Jessica frowned. She was tired of being made fun of just because she didn't happen to be a millionaire! Maybe she wasn't the best at managing what little money she did have, but they didn't have to rub it in constantly. Janet and Lila thought they were so much better than her just because they had money in their wallets. Jessica didn't even *have* a wallet. The way things were going, she didn't exactly need one, either.

"Jessica, we could have lent you the extra money for the regular-size sundae," Janet said as Joe set down their orders on the table. Jessica's sundae looked like something from the kiddie menu compared to theirs.

"Yeah, sure," Jessica muttered. "And then you guys would hold it over my head for a week."

"No we wouldn't," Lila said. She scooped up an enormous spoonful of ice cream. "A few days, tops. Mmm . . . this is so huge, I don't know if I'll be able to finish it."

As Lila and Janet started giggling again, Jessica mashed the smidgen of whipped cream on top of her sundae, trying to spread it out. Why did they have to act so superior all the time? Well, she knew something *they* didn't know. "Money isn't everything," she muttered. "I mean, look at Brian Boyd."

Lila raised one eyebrow. "What about him?" she asked.

Jessica cleared her throat. "He might have a lot of money, but that doesn't mean he has a good life."

"Why not?" Janet asked.

"Yeah. He does have a mansion and a pool that's almost as nice as mine," Lila said.

Jessica bit her lip. She didn't want to break her promise to Elizabeth, but this was almost too good a secret to keep to herself. Anyway, everyone was going to know sooner or later that Brian wasn't living at home anymore. He'd probably tell everyone—he'd probably even brag about being taken away by the police, knowing him. "Sure, he has a lot of stuff," Jessica said. "But look at his home life."

"Jessica, what are you talking about? What do you know about Brian's home life?" Lila asked.

"Brian's in trouble," Jessica said, trying to sound mysterious. "Real trouble, you guys."

"Yeah, at school," Janet said. "He has enough detentions lined up to last at least a month."

"It's not school," Jessica said. "There was this huge article about him in the paper today." It wasn't actually *huge*, but she had to make it sound good.

"There *was*?" Lila's eyes widened. "Why?"

"He had to move out of his parents' house," Jessica said, pleased to be the one with the news.

"Can you believe it? The police came and actually took him away."

"You're kidding!" Janet exclaimed. "Because he was getting into so many fights?"

Jessica shook her head. "No. He wasn't *in* any fights—at least, not with anyone we know. It was his parents."

"His parents?" Lila asked, looking confused.

"Look, I don't know the whole story," Jessica said quickly. "But something happened at his house, and the police took Brian and put him in foster care or whatever. And now the whole family's being, like . . . investigated. And charges might be filed and stuff."

"Wow," Janet said. She looked completely stunned.

Jessica shifted in her seat. Somehow, showing up Lila and Janet didn't feel as good as she'd thought it would. She was already regretting that she'd blurted out the secret. Elizabeth would be furious if she ever found out.

Lila dabbed the corners of her mouth with a napkin. "Well, I'm not surprised. Brian's always been in trouble."

"Yeah, but this is different." Jessica frowned. She had a feeling that Lila and Janet hadn't quite understood what she was telling them. But maybe it was better that way. Especially since she felt like she shouldn't have told them in the first place.

It's better to keep things vague, she decided. *Just in case it's not Brian.* She took another bite of her rapidly disappearing miniature sundae.

At least she'd gotten everyone to stop talking about how broke she was!

On Monday morning, Elizabeth waited as long as she could outside school. She wanted a chance to talk to Brian before school started. She wasn't positive that Saturday's article was about him, and she was hoping as hard as she could that it wasn't. But she couldn't imagine who else it could be. She was pretty sure nobody else in town had had the police at their house last Thursday night.

Every time she tried to tell herself it must be someone else, the image of Brian crying in the alley that night popped into her head. Then she got this horrible feeling that it had to be him.

And if it *was* Brian, she wanted him to know that if he needed a place to stay, he could stay at their house. Even if she hadn't asked her parents yet, she was sure they'd say yes. They'd understand. It was an emergency.

Finally, a minute before the final bell was supposed to ring, Brian came into view on his mountain bike. He locked his bike to the rack and walked toward Elizabeth.

"Brian?" she said tentatively.

"What do you want?" he replied.

Elizabeth looked at him nervously. She didn't

know what she was afraid of, but she definitely felt uneasy.

"I was wondering," Elizabeth said. "You know, if you needed anything."

"I don't need any more Girl Scout cookies this year, OK, Miss Goody-Goody?" Brian scoffed, flicking his hair back. "So leave me alone."

"Are you sure you don't need anything?" Elizabeth asked, deciding to ignore his rude comment. "I thought maybe you could use . . . someone to talk to. I mean, I know we don't know each other that well, but . . . if you need something, like a place to stay—"

"Why would I need a place to stay?" Brian retorted, staring at Elizabeth.

"I'm not saying you do, but—"

"Good, because I don't need any *help,* from you or anyone else," Brian said angrily. "If you're so anxious to help someone, why don't you go tell your loser friends over there to stop staring at me? I mean, what is everyone's problem today?" He stormed past Elizabeth into the building.

She looked over at Amy and Maria, who were just outside the building, watching Brian as he yanked open the front door. *Don't tell me they know about the article, too,* Elizabeth thought with a sense of panic. Did everyone know about Brian's problem?

But if Brian was the person in the article, then why was he acting as if everything was just the same—as if nothing strange was going on? All she'd wanted was to offer him some help. *Why do I even bother trying? Once a jerk, always a jerk,* she told herself.

But for the first time since she had met Brian, Elizabeth didn't quite believe that.

"Did you hear?" Maria asked as she slid into the seat next to Elizabeth for English class.

"Hear what?" Elizabeth asked.

"About Brian," Maria whispered. "About how he has to go live somewhere else now. Everyone's talking about it!"

Elizabeth's chest tightened. "Really?" She wondered how everyone else knew. Jessica had promised not to tell. "How did you find out?" she asked Maria.

"It's all over the school. Everyone's talking about it," Maria said.

Elizabeth bit her lip. Maria's knowing was one thing, but everyone knowing . . . it would be so embarrassing for Brian to have his private problems discussed in public like that. But she was sort of glad to be able to talk about it with a friend and not keep it all hidden inside. "Isn't it the most awful thing you've ever heard? I feel so sorry for him," she told Maria in a soft voice.

"Sorry for him?" Maria repeated. "That's a laugh."

"What?" Elizabeth was shocked. "Maria, I know you don't like Brian, especially after how he made fun of you the other day—"

"Try *every* day!" Maria commented.

"OK, he can be a real bully when he wants to be," Elizabeth admitted. "And I'm not that close to him or anything, but come on—nobody deserves what he's been through."

Maria sighed impatiently. "Elizabeth, what *he's* been through? How about what his parents have been through? He's constantly in trouble, and that's why he's getting moved out of his house, because he's uncontrollable and—"

"No, that's not it at all," Elizabeth argued. "It's his parents who—"

Maria put her hand on Elizabeth's arm and squeezed tightly. "Shh . . . somebody's coming."

Elizabeth glanced toward the door. A hush fell over the classroom when Brian walked in. It was as if everyone had stopped talking because they'd been talking about Brian. Elizabeth felt immediately guilty, as if she'd been caught doing something wrong.

"Glad you could join us today," Mr. Bowman said, smiling at Brian.

Elizabeth glanced at her teacher with surprise. *Does Mr. Bowman know, too?* she wondered. *He'd have to; he's one of Brian's teachers.* Suddenly she felt as if the whole situation had gotten way out of hand.

Brian didn't look at Mr. Bowman as he walked to his desk. He glanced around the room at the guys he usually spoke to, but he didn't say hello, and neither did they. The room was even more quiet than it was during a test. Brian slid into a seat

in front of Elizabeth. She felt such a pang of sympa-
thy for him, for what he'd been through and the
fact that everyone in school knew about it, that she
almost started crying.

"OK, class," Mr. Bowman said. He smiled, but
Elizabeth could tell from his shaking voice that he
felt as nervous and upset as she did. "Today is
Monday, which means . . ."—he stared at his
notes—"we'll be talking about blended families
and, let's see . . . the role of foster families in
today's society." He cleared his throat and glanced
uneasily at Brian, who was busy unpacking his
backpack. "Now that I think about it, I'm not sure
we can cover all that in one day. How about if we
just stick with blended families?"

Six

◇

You good-for-nothing little brat. You think you can have everything you want, don't you? Well, you can't. You don't deserve anything! His father's words had been echoing in Brian's head all morning. Now, as he walked down the hall toward lunch, he kept remembering the last fight they'd had, one of their worst ever. His father had said terrible things, things that Brian would never be able to forget.

Everything you have, I worked for, do you hear me? And that's how you pay me back, by messing up? Then his father struck him and shoved him against the wall. His arm was still sore. It had hurt Brian all through gym, every time he took a shot.

Brian was by himself now, which was just the way he wanted it. After gym class, he'd stayed out on the basketball court to take some extra free-throw practice. He had come into the locker room late, after everyone else. When he walked in, he'd overheard several guys talking about him.

The same thing had happened when he walked into English class, and math . . . It seemed like everywhere he went, people were talking and staring. He was getting really sick of being the topic of conversation. Didn't they have anything better to do? It was getting on his nerves.

The fact that he'd barely gotten any sleep the last few nights didn't help. It was impossible to sleep in that children's center with a bunch of other kids around, all wanting to know his story. He didn't feel like talking about his *story*. And he definitely didn't want to hear theirs. They didn't know him. They could never understand.

Brian yanked open the cafeteria door. As he walked over to pick up a tray, he again felt as if everyone was staring at him. Sure, they tried to look casual about it, but they were looking. He picked up some food as quickly as he could and headed for a table in the corner.

"Hey, Brian!" Ken called to him, grabbing Brian's sleeve as he walked past a table where Ken, Todd, and Aaron Dallas were sitting.

"Oh . . . hey." Brian tried to sound casual. But he hadn't spoken to anyone all day except that nosy Elizabeth Wakefield, and his voice came out in a tiny croak.

"Dude, have a seat." Aaron pointed to an empty chair.

"Yeah," Todd added.

Why are these guys being so nice to me? Brian wondered. He was usually the one forcing them to talk to him. "OK," he said slowly. "I mean, sure."

Maybe it'll be cool to hang out with the guys, he thought as he slid into a seat at their table. They probably wouldn't bug him about anything. He cut a piece of lasagna and lifted it to his mouth. The only problem was, he wasn't that hungry. He hadn't been for days. Ever since . . . it happened. "So, what's up with you guys?" he asked.

"Not much," Ken said. "Hey—I got that new college football video game. You've got to come over and play it sometime."

"You mean, show *you* how to play it?" Brian teased. He was starting to relax. It was such a relief to be sitting around and joking. Everything had been so serious lately; he needed a break.

Ken laughed. "Yeah, OK. I can't understand, like, half of it, and I've read the directions about ten times. Maybe you could come over this afternoon."

"No," Brian said quickly. "I can't."

"Oh. Well, whenever," Ken said.

"It's just that I . . . have some extra homework to catch up on," Brian said hastily. He wasn't going to tell them that the place where he was temporarily staying required that he come home right after school to do his homework in a supervised study period. As far as he was concerned, the less said about that place, the better.

"Oh. Well, that's cool," Aaron said.

"Homework—cool? Not exactly," Brian joked.

Aaron and Ken both laughed, but they looked a little uneasy. Todd just kept staring at Brian, with a concerned expression on his face.

Then Todd cleared his throat. "So . . . I know you have the homework thing covered, but, uh . . . is everything else OK?"

"Sure." Brian shrugged. He didn't like the way Todd sounded, as if there were something to worry about. "Everything's cool."

"Really?" Todd asked. "I mean . . . I heard about what happened. You know."

"No," Brian said, feeling his heart start to pound harder. So even these guys just couldn't leave him alone. "Why don't *you* tell me what *happened*?" He stared angrily at Todd.

"Come on, Brian, don't be mad," Ken said. "You can talk to us, you know?"

"Yeah, you don't have to pretend that everything's OK," Aaron said. "I mean, maybe we haven't always gotten along or whatever, but that doesn't mean we can't be your friends now. And if you need anything . . ."

"Why would I need anything from you?" Brian demanded harshly. First Elizabeth Wakefield, now these jerks—everyone kept offering their *help*. As if they could help! They didn't know anything!

"Look, all I meant was, maybe we could do something," Aaron said.

"Yeah, we were talking about it," Ken began, "and—"

"Will everyone quit *talking* about it!" Brian cried. He stood up, shoving the table away from him. Before he realized what was happening, the whole table fell over. Trays, cups, and silverware clattered onto the floor.

Ken jumped up and stared at Brian, milk dripping off his shirt. Todd reached out, trying to grab Brian's arm. "Hey, take it easy," Todd said. "We only want to help you."

Brian looked around and he saw that the entire cafeteria was staring at him. He hadn't meant to knock over the table—he just wanted to get out of there and get everyone off his back. "Well, forget it," he said, his voice catching in his throat. "Because you can't help."

Just as he turned to walk away, Mr. Clark strode over, blocking his path. "Brian, what seems to be the problem here?"

The problem? The problem is that I just need everyone to leave me alone! Brian thought. Because if people kept being so nice to him, he was going to fall apart. And he couldn't let that happen—not now. Not ever.

"What was that all about?" Amy asked, looking over at where Brian was standing by the up-turned table.

Elizabeth watched as a glass rolled off the capsized table and crashed to the floor before either Todd or Aaron could catch it. "I—I don't know," she said. Looking over at Brian, she saw Mr. Clark approach him. The two of them walked out of the cafeteria a moment later.

"Guess he's in big trouble now," Amy commented, sounding sad.

"You mean *again*," Maria said. "Look at Todd—he's in total shock. Of course, I would be, too, if someone knocked over the table I was eating on."

"Maybe it was an accident," Amy suggested quietly.

"An accident? Yeah, right," Maria said. "As if you could knock over one of these tables by accident. Anyway, he looked really mad—you saw him!"

Elizabeth could barely listen to her friends' argument; she was too concerned about Brian. But Maria was right—nobody just knocked over a table. Brian must have done it on purpose. But why? Had one of the guys said something to upset him?

"All I can say is, I hope Mr. Clark suspends him this time," Maria said. "Never mind suspend, how about expel? Brian doesn't even belong here, not after all the—"

"Maria, you don't know the whole story!" Elizabeth interrupted.

"I know enough," Maria insisted. "I know Brian's been an utter jerk ever since he moved here, and look what he's done now." She glanced at the table, which a cafeteria worker was now righting and cleaning off. "He's a troublemaker."

"Well, maybe Brian has bigger problems than we know right now," Elizabeth said. "Why don't you give him a break?"

"Give him a break?" Maria scoffed. "Oh, that's a good one, Elizabeth."

"But I mean—oh, never mind," Elizabeth said, shaking her head. She couldn't convince Maria that Brian might need their compassion right now. It was hopeless.

"You realize, of course, that I'll have to notify somebody of your behavior," Mr. Clark informed Brian once they reached his office. *Notify somebody,* Brian thought. *Only there's nobody.* He shifted uncomfortably in his chair.

"Brian, I wish I didn't have to do this," Mr. Clark said. "I know you're having a rough time. And things aren't easy right now. But that doesn't give you the right to disrupt other students' lives. I won't stand for those kinds of outbursts in our school."

"But I—," Brian began, then broke off. What was the use of trying to explain that he hadn't meant to hurt anyone, that he'd only wanted to escape? As much as he apologized, Mr. Clark probably wouldn't believe him. The way he'd been acting lately, nobody would believe that he didn't really mean any of it. He couldn't blame them.

"Yes?" Mr. Clark asked. "Did you want to say something, Brian?" He looked patiently across his desk at Brian.

Brian fiddled with a piece of upholstery that was starting to come off the chair. He could tell Mr. Clark all about the huge fight with his father that was so loud, the neighbors had called the police. He could describe the way his father chased him into the yard, and how he'd almost run right into the police car when it pulled up in their driveway. But Mr. Clark wouldn't understand.

Besides, the details of what had happened were Brian's secret—the only thing no one else knew about. Even if Mr. Clark knew some of what happened, he didn't know the whole truth. And nobody ever could—it was too horrible.

And too humiliating.

"No, I don't have anything to say," Brian said gruffly.

"Well, in that case . . . do you know the number of the new house you're staying at?" Mr. Clark asked.

"Oh. Yeah," Brian replied.

"Good, then I'll just call and explain that although you're not being suspended this time, the next time anything like this occurs, I will be forced to give you a three-day suspension. Is that clear?"

Brian nodded. He wrote down the number of the pay phone at the Sweet Valley Video Arcade. Nobody ever answered the phone there, and giving out the phone number to teachers, parents, and principals was kind of a running joke. "Here. This is the number of my new foster family's house. You know, they're really great."

"Are they?" Mr. Clark smiled. "That's good news."

"Yeah," Brian said, standing up to leave. "They've been waiting for a kid for a long time, I guess. I mean, you should see my room. I have everything there."

"Well, I'm glad to hear that," Mr. Clark said, nodding. "Brian, you will come talk to me—or somebody in guidance—if it doesn't work out?"

Brian frowned. Why did Mr. Clark think that it wouldn't work out? He was acting like it was Brian's fault that he had to leave home.

The same way his father always acted. Like Brian was the one who was making his father's life and everything around them go wrong. But that wasn't true.

Was it?

Elizabeth stared at the list of upcoming events on the social page of that week's edition of the *Sixers*. She had to get the issue done by Tuesday, which meant she had to finish typing it that afternoon. But she was missing one event: the date for the school trip to the aquarium.

She decided to go to Mr. Clark's office and find out which day the school trip was planned for.

She left the *Sixers* office and headed down the hall to the principal's office. As she walked in, she passed a couple of women apparently waiting to meet with Mr. Clark. They were talking in hushed, angry tones. As she got closer to the secretary's desk, she overheard what they were saying.

"Well, that's just the point," one woman said. "The apple doesn't fall far from the tree. One minute it's a fight with his father, and then today I hear he's throwing furniture around—"

"Have some compassion," the other woman argued. "You've got to understand what that young boy is going through!"

"I don't understand," the first woman said. "And I don't want that troublemaker in the same school as my daughter."

"But don't you see, he's probably so upset that he doesn't know what he's doing. A classic symptom of child abuse is—"

Elizabeth stepped away from the two women, not wanting to hear any more. She turned toward Mrs. Knight to check on the field trip date. But at the moment, the secretary was busy talking on the phone; she seemed to be fielding several calls at once.

"Yes, I understand your concerns, but Mr. Clark is handling the situation in the best way he can," she explained. She clicked onto another line. "Hello, may I help you? Yes. Yes, we're very aware of the situation. I'm not at liberty to give out that information. However, I can tell you that the student in question is safe. Thank you for your concern. Yes, child abuse is a terrible crime." Mrs. Knight hung up and picked up another call.

Child abuse. Child abuse. The words made Elizabeth feel sick to her stomach. When she'd read about it in the paper on Saturday, it sounded so formal and unreal, like something that would never touch her life. And now everyone was saying it, over and over, and she couldn't get the words out of her head. *Abuse. Brian's being abused.*

Elizabeth stepped away from the counter, trembling. She walked unsteadily down the hall, then she started running, as fast as she could, straight out the front door, without even collecting her backpack from the *Sixers* office.

Seven

"I still can't believe what happened today at lunch," Mandy Miller said that afternoon as she dangled her feet in Lila's backyard pool. "Can you guys?"

Jessica smoothed sunblock onto her arms. "I know things are rough, but Brian didn't have to dump that table all over Todd and Aaron—"

"Can you believe the nerve?" Grace Oliver said.

"If I'd been sitting at that table and he had spilled food all over me . . ." Janet shook her head. "I would have made sure he got suspended—for the rest of the year."

"Not me," Ellen said. "I would have started a food fight!"

"Well, all I can say is, the less I have to deal with Brian Boyd, the better." Lila swept her long brown hair over her shoulder. "I mean, after what we all know about him . . . I'm surprised he even showed up at school today."

Jessica shifted uneasily on the edge of the pool. She had been surprised that Brian had come to school, but only because she wouldn't have wanted to come to school if everyone was talking about her. "Well, maybe he didn't have anywhere else to go," she suggested.

"Let's talk about something else," Janet said, quickly dismissing Jessica's comment. "Brian gets enough attention at school—we don't have to talk about him all afternoon, too!"

"Yeah, I think that's why he does the stuff he does," Lila said. "He's not happy unless he's the center of attention."

"I'm not sure if that's why," Mandy said, looking concerned.

"Yeah, it's not like Brian's having fun," Jessica said. "I mean, whatever happened in his family, I'm sure it's not a great thing to have to deal with."

"Well, I say he deserves it," Grace declared.

Jessica looked at Grace with surprise. *Deserves it? Why does she think that?* It seemed to her that her friends weren't being very understanding. "Did you guys get the story wrong or something?" she asked.

Grace turned to her and shrugged. "No. Why?"

"Brian's a jerk. End of story," Janet declared.

Jessica stared at the rippling pool water. *Brian might be a jerk. But maybe he has his reasons.*

Still, she didn't want to think about it all afternoon; she was at Lila's to have fun. And nobody else seemed too bothered by the situation.

Maybe I'm just overreacting, she told herself. *Things will work out for Brian, if they haven't already.*

"Oh, my gosh—I almost forgot!" Lila cried later that afternoon as everyone gathered their towels to go home. "I mentioned to my dad that the season finale of *Snob Hill 90214* is on this Thursday—and guess what he said!"

"'Great—what time is it on?'" Mandy joked.

Jessica laughed, wrapping her beach towel around her waist. "Can you imagine Mr. Fowler watching *Snob Hill*?"

"He hates that show," Lila said, smiling. "'All those young men look like they need to wash their hair,'" she said in a deep voice, imitating her father. "'And what about those sideburns, could they be any longer?'"

Janet laughed. "You must admit, your dad is hopelessly square."

"Like yours is any better," Lila said, giggling. "Your mother still likes disco music!"

"So does mine," Grace admitted. "She has, like . . . records. On vinyl. And she's proud of it!"

"Well, getting back to the important part of this, I asked my father if I could have a season finale party *and* sleepover—I'm calling it Snob Hill Night!" Lila announced.

"That sounds great!" Jessica said enthusiastically.

Then she remembered: She wasn't allowed to go to sleepovers on school nights. "Is that on Thursday?"

"Duh," Janet said, rolling her eyes. "The show's only been on that night for three years."

"Right," Jessica said, feeling her face turn pink. "Of course." *Couldn't they change the schedule once in a while?* "I just hope that's not, you know, a problem for anyone."

"I know I can go," Janet said with a shrug.

"Me, too. As long as I get all my homework done before I leave the house," Mandy said. "My mother actually checks."

"I'll have to make sure, but I think Thursdays are OK," Grace said. "Since there's only one more school day to deal with."

"Then it's settled!" Lila said. "You guys will all come over Thursday—we'll have a huge party, with tons of munchies, and we'll watch the show! Doesn't that sound great?"

"Great," Jessica muttered under her breath, snapping shut the top on the bottle of lotion.

Lila looked at her. "What's the problem, Jessica?"

"Oh, umm . . . nothing! There's no problem," Jessica declared.

"Are you sure?" Lila asked. "You will be able to come, won't you?"

"Sure," Jessica bluffed. "No problem. It's just—I have to ask my parents first. I'm sure they'll say yes, though." Jessica knew they wouldn't like the idea, but maybe there was some way she could convince them.

Sure. If I learn how to do hypnosis.

"Uh-huh," Lila said, sounding skeptical. "Well, let me know tomorrow so I can tell my dad who's coming."

"Oh, sure," Jessica said with a weak smile. "I'll let you know tomorrow morning. But you can count me in already. I mean, it's practically a done deal."

Practically. But not actually.

Brian leaned his bike against a tree in the city park. He'd been riding around all afternoon, trying to put off going back to the "safe house" where he was supposed to be staying. Some house. It was more like an infirmary—one big room with a bunch of cots.

He was already an hour late for study period, and he didn't care. *What are they going to do to me? Kick me out? They'd be doing me a favor.*

Brian was supposed to stay at the juvenile safe house only until they found a foster family for him. Which, they'd told him, could take a few days—or a few weeks. Maybe even a few months.

He kicked at an old tennis ball someone had left on the ground. It had probably been hit out of the courts by the park entrance, he decided. When he had been learning to play, he'd hit balls out of the court all the time. He'd always thought that was how you made the best shots, by hitting the ball as hard as you could. It looked that way when he watched tennis matches on television, anyway. His father had taught him how to play tennis, just like he'd taught him football, soccer . . . everything. He'd taught Brian how to concentrate during a match and how to control his shots.

Control. That was a laugh, Brian thought. His dad didn't even know the meaning of control now. Brian sank down onto the grass, leaning back against the tree.

Things used to be so different. He picked up the ball and tossed it as far as he could, watching it sail through the air and bounce lightly on the ground. He used to spend tons of time with his father, and it used to be fun.

Until Mr. Boyd made a bad decision on a big business deal a couple of years before and his company in Los Angeles put him on probation. Then he started to turn into a different person. A mean, angry person. His company gave him more and more warnings. And the worse things got at work, the angrier Mr. Boyd was at home.

Finally the company fired Brian's dad. The Boyds moved to Sweet Valley so his dad could get a new start. But instead he'd had to take a lower-level job like the one he used to have seven or eight years ago. His work had always been really important to him, and now his father hated his job. Instead of working extra hard to get ahead, or looking for another, better job, Brian's father decided to take his frustrations out on his son.

And his mother . . . she wasn't doing any better since their move. At first she'd tried to stop his father. But she couldn't, not when he was really angry. So she'd started drinking. First just a drink or two. Then several drinks. Then bottles started appearing in the cupboards—and just as quickly in the recycling bin, empty.

Brian felt like both of his parents had given up on life. And in the process, given up on him. His father used to tell him what a great kid he was . . . how proud he was of Brian . . .

Now all he did was yell at Brian for being such a disappointment. No matter what Brian said or did, it was wrong. And his father didn't only yell. He hit. Hard.

Brian could hardly remember what it felt like to be part of a happy family. Now it felt as though he didn't belong anywhere. He had nowhere to go. And nobody cared about him anymore . . . especially not his parents.

Sure, they'd cried and begged forgiveness when the police had come to take him away. But they always did that—it didn't mean a thing.

What's the point in even looking for another family for me to live with? It's not like they'll want me, either.

Nobody does.

Elizabeth was running as fast as she could. She wanted to get home. Why was it so hard? She kept pushing herself, telling her legs to move, but it was as if her feet were stuck in cement.

She glanced over her shoulder. Two figures were running after her; the sun in the sky behind them made it impossible for Elizabeth to see who they were. Their running figures cast long, eerie shadows on the street behind her. "No," she gasped. "They can't catch me— they can't!"

Elizabeth turned back around and kept running, sprinting hard, her lungs gasping for air with each step. Behind her, she heard footsteps.

I can't let them catch me! she thought, panicked. They'll hurt me—the same way they hurt Brian! She glanced over her shoulder and saw Mr. and Mrs. Boyd coming toward her, their arms outstretched. "No!" she screamed. "Stay away from me!"

Brian's parents came closer, laughing at her, their cackling voices echoing on the darkened street.

I have to get away from them. I have to run faster, I have to—Elizabeth's foot slipped on a branch in the street and she started falling to the ground—only it seemed like it was taking forever to fall, and on the way down, she looked up again—

The people reaching out for her weren't Mr. and Mrs. Boyd—they were her mother and father!

"No—don't! Mom and Dad, no!" Elizabeth cried just as her back smashed against the pavement.

The next thing Elizabeth knew, somebody was shaking her arm. "Honey, are you OK? Elizabeth, wake up—you were just having a bad dream."

Elizabeth slowly opened her eyes. When she saw her mother and father leaning over the bed, she instinctively grabbed the sheets and pulled them more tightly around her.

"Elizabeth? Honey, you were yelling in your sleep," her mother said. "Are you all right?"

"There's nothing to be afraid of." Her father sat on the bed. "We're right here."

With a jolt, Elizabeth remembered what she had just been dreaming. She sat up in bed, shuddering. "Oh, Mom. It was terrible. I had this nightmare that . . ." Elizabeth's voice caught in her throat. "I can't even tell you, it's so horrible!" She felt a tear roll down her cheek.

"It was just a dream." Her father reached out and hugged Elizabeth tightly. "It's all over now."

"No," Elizabeth said, shaking her head, "it isn't."

"What do you mean?" her mother asked.

"Why don't you come downstairs, have a snack with us, and you can tell us all about your dream," her father suggested.

Elizabeth nodded. "OK. Actually, it has to do with something I thought you guys might already know about—what happened to Brian Boyd."

Her parents looked at each other, then turned back to Elizabeth and shrugged. "I haven't heard anything. But I have been busy with that special project at work," her mother said.

"I haven't heard anything either," her father

said. "What about Brian? Is he all right?"

"N-not really, no," Elizabeth said, slipping her robe on over her pajamas. "I'll tell you as much as I know."

Mrs. Wakefield shook her head. "I can't believe this. Nobody deserves to be hurt by their parents. Nobody."

"I know." Elizabeth nodded. She and her parents were sitting on the living room couch, huddled close together. She had just told them everything that had happened over the past week or so, including seeing Brian crying that night in the alley.

"How's everyone at school taking it?" Mr. Wakefield asked, sounding concerned.

"Not that great," Elizabeth said. "I mean, I'm really upset for Brian. But some people—even Maria—think it's his fault or something."

Mrs. Wakefield looked astonished. "Why would they think that?"

"Well, Brian's never been very popular," Elizabeth explained. "He's been mean to some kids, sort of like a bully. And he's kind of a know-it-all. So everyone's kind of decided that he must be the one who's done something wrong."

"Well, they're probably just scared . . . like you," her mother said. "Only they're reacting differently."

"I guess," Elizabeth said. "But it just seems so unfair! I mean, what's Brian supposed to do? I don't even know where he's living now. And what about his parents? Are they going to get him back someday?"

Mr. Wakefield cleared his throat. "I know from all the time I spend at the courthouse that this happens to a lot of kids. More than you'd imagine, actually." He took a deep breath. "And I see custody cases all the time that involve parents who've mistreated their children—and then end up getting them back." He shook his head. "It makes me sick."

"You don't think that would happen with the Boyds, do you?" Elizabeth asked, horrified. "I mean . . . if they're bad to him, he can't go back there! Tell me he won't!"

"Calm down, sweetie," Mrs. Wakefield said, stroking her hair soothingly. "I'm sure Brian will be placed with a nice, kind foster family. No judge would send him back home, at least not until his parents work out their problems."

"But what if the judge doesn't believe Brian?" Elizabeth asked. "What if—"

"Honey, you've got to stop worrying about this," Mr. Wakefield said. "It will work out. And as much as you want to help Brian, you simply can't right now."

"I know," Elizabeth said, starting to cry again. "And that's what makes it so horrible."

"Just because you can't help him, doesn't mean he won't get the help he needs," her mother said, squeezing Elizabeth in a hug. "Things will get better for Brian. I'd say that the worst is over."

Elizabeth nodded, drying her eyes on the sleeve of her mother's terry cloth robe. "I hope so," she said.

"Now, how about if you go upstairs and lie down—read for a while if you want to," Mr. Wakefield recommended. "Don't think about falling asleep—when you get tired enough, you will. And no more nightmares!"

"OK. If you say so." Elizabeth smiled at her father through her tears. Her parents kissed her, and Elizabeth trudged upstairs to her room. She slipped back under the covers and got out her favorite book of poems. Whenever she had trouble sleeping, she read from that book—it always calmed her down, even though some of the poems were sad.

She was flipping through the pages, looking for a good place to start, when she heard her parents coming upstairs. They were whispering, but they weren't being very quiet about it.

"Well, I feel just as badly as you do, Ned," her mother said.

"I've never seen Elizabeth so upset," her father replied. "This is really getting to her!"

"I know," Mrs. Wakefield said. "And I know we can't shield the kids from everything, but sometimes I wish we could just shut out the rest of the world."

"So do I, Alice," Mr. Wakefield said with a sigh, pausing outside Elizabeth's door briefly. She held her breath, not wanting them to know she'd overheard. "So do I," he whispered.

"Ned . . . we have to make sure that boy gets the

help he needs," Elizabeth's mother said as they continued down the hall.

"We will," her father answered. "That boy needs people on his side."

He sure does, Elizabeth thought. Maybe Brian didn't want her help. And maybe there was nothing she could do.

But if there ever was, she'd be the first to do it. She'd do anything to keep him from getting hurt again. Anything.

Eight

◇

"Mom? Can I ask you something?" Jessica said at breakfast on Tuesday morning.

"Sure," her mother replied. "What is it?"

"Well, umm . . ." Jessica glanced around the table. Why did everyone seem so out of it? Elizabeth looked like she hadn't slept very well lately, and her parents both looked so concerned and serious. Only Steven was acting normal, eating about four slices of toast. Maybe now wasn't the best time to ask her parents about Lila's slumber party—but she had to find out before school so she could tell Lila to expect her. "I was wondering if I could go to Lila's house Thursday night."

"Why?" Mrs. Wakefield asked.

"For a party. For this show we love—you know, *Snob Hill 90214?*" Jessica said.

"The show with the guys and girls who think they're really cool," Steven added. "And they all run around in bathing suits all the time."

"It deals with important issues," Jessica protested.

"Like shopping and dating," Steven commented.

Jessica stuck out her tongue at him. "Anyway, Mom, the point is that Lila's having this sleepover party—"

"Sleep over? On a Thursday night? No, Jessica— I'm sorry, but you know that's against the rules," her mother said, shaking her head.

"But, Mom . . . it's a big party," Jessica argued. "All the other Unicorns are going to be there, and *their* parents think it's OK."

"You know our rules," her father said. "We can't change them—"

"But Dad, it's the season *finale*," Jessica argued.

"Oh, my gosh!" Steven slapped his forehead with the palm of his hand. "The finale! How will I live without a new show every week?"

"And if we don't all watch it together, it won't be the same," Jessica said, frowning at Steven. She hastily tried to think of another way she could get through to her parents. "It's important for parents to let their children experience things for themselves, Mr. Bowman told us. If I end up staying up too late and being tired on Friday, then I'll, like, learn a lesson, and then you won't have to convince me that this rule makes sense the next time I ask." She smiled triumphantly.

Her mother smiled weakly and shook her head. "Nice try, Jessica, but no."

"But—every time I can't do what everyone else is doing, it's really bad for my self-image," Jessica said. "And parents need to trust their children. And—"

"Jessica, you're not going to Lila's for the sleep-over party Thursday night, and that's final!" Mrs. Wakefield snapped. "I want both you girls home with me for the next few days."

Jessica gave her mother a puzzled look. "Why?"

"I just do." Mrs. Wakefield stood up and brushed a few crumbs off the kitchen table into her hand.

"Mom . . . you're totally stifling my individuality, do you know that?" Jessica asked.

"There are more important things in life than your individuality," Mrs. Wakefield said sternly. "In fact, this is a time when families need to stick together."

Jessica frowned. What in the world was her mother talking about? Well, she didn't have time to figure it out. Her essay for Mr. Bowman was due tomorrow morning, and she had plenty of new material to put into it!

Being good parents means letting your daughter go to parties with her friends, she thought. *Definitely.*

Why did her mother look so worried, anyway? And Elizabeth hadn't even defended her. What was happening to her family?

Brian tossed his gym clothes into his locker and closed the door. Everyone was rushing to the cafeteria, but Brian didn't feel like going back there, not after what had happened yesterday. Besides, he wasn't hungry.

He headed out of the locker room and upstairs to the school library. He hadn't been getting any of his homework done lately, and he wanted to use lunch period to work on his essay for Mr. Bowman's class, which was due the next day.

He sat down at a desk in the corner of the library, as far away from everyone else as possible. Nobody seemed to be talking about him anymore, but nobody was talking *to* him, either. Everyone was acting as if he had some kind of disease they didn't want to catch. Brian couldn't blame them—he'd probably act the same way toward anyone else.

He pulled out a notebook and opened it to a fresh page. As he thought about Mr. Bowman's assignment, the library door opened. When Elizabeth Wakefield walked in, Brian felt like slinking under his desk. Elizabeth Wakefield. She wasn't looking for him, was she? He didn't want to talk to her. Ever since she'd caught him crying that night, he'd felt completely embarrassed whenever she was around, even though she had never brought it up. Besides, she was such a goody-goody, all the teachers loved her to death. She wasn't somebody Brian exactly wanted to be friends with. Her idea of a fun time was probably studying. *I bet she finished her dumb essay weeks ago—before it was even assigned.*

Please don't stop to talk to me, Brian thought as

Elizabeth came closer. *I'm not in the mood.*

But Elizabeth walked right past Brian to a table behind him, only giving him a slight smile as she went by. He couldn't believe she could still smile at him, not after the way he'd yelled at her the past few times she had approached him.

Brian took the cap off of a pen and stared at the blank sheet in front of him. *Write about my parents? But how?*

The assignment was to write about what made a family into a family; what made a house a home; what worked and what didn't. Brian didn't know what worked—but he knew what didn't. And he knew how a family could go from being great to being . . . a nightmare. Would Mr. Bowman really want to know all that?

It's the only thing I can write about, whether he likes it or not. Besides, Brian didn't plan on winning any contests. He just wanted to make sure he passed his classes, or he'd have even more problems to deal with.

Behind him, he heard Elizabeth's pen scratching against paper. *If she's still writing her essay,* Brian thought, *hers is probably about how wonderful it is to be an identical twin and how much her family loved one another.*

But that wasn't how all families worked. Brian wanted Mr. Bowman to know that. Mr. Bowman was an OK teacher, and he was really smart, but there were some things he didn't know. Like when Brian came into school with all those bruises, week after week . . . Mr. Bowman should have noticed.

But he hadn't. Nobody had.

"I can't believe this many people showed up!" Maria said on Tuesday night. "Mr. Clark only announced the meeting this morning!"

"It's an emergency situation," Elizabeth reminded her. "That's why everyone's here." She looked around the crowded school auditorium, noticing that all of her friends' parents had managed to come to the emergency PTA meeting Mr. Clark had hastily arranged. She and Maria would serve as the two student representatives to the Parents and Teachers Association.

"Attention, everyone." Mr. Clark tapped the microphone. "Can we get started?"

People stopped talking, and everyone stared up at the stage.

"I called this meeting, as you know, because of a situation that developed recently and that affects one of our students," Mr. Clark began. "Let me start with a brief overview of things, in case everyone doesn't have the same information.

"After several reports of domestic disturbances at a home in Sweet Valley, a student was removed from the home, so that the state could investigate potential child abuse. The state's preliminary investigation has shown that the child shall not be returned to the home, and that the parents will be charged with endangering his life."

Elizabeth looked at Maria, putting her hand over her mouth. Brian's life was at stake! It was even worse than she'd ever imagined.

"In a situation like this, the first priority is to establish the child in a safe, supportive foster family," Mr. Clark explained. "While the social workers have not yet located a permanent home for this student—"

"And they're not going to!" somebody in the crowd shouted.

Mr. Clark lowered his reading glasses on his nose and looked out at the audience. "Excuse me?"

A man Elizabeth didn't recognize stood up. "That child you're talking about is trouble. No one in town would take him in—and I for one am glad!"

A few people in the crowd murmured in agreement.

Mr. Clark cleared his throat. "What are you saying?"

"Mr. Clark, we don't want Brian Boyd in this school anymore," the man said. He was the first to mention Brian's name.

Elizabeth felt her heart race with anxiety and confusion. What was the man talking about? And why did he have to call Brian by name? Even the newspaper didn't use kids' names, and for a good reason—to protect their privacy.

"He's been nothing but trouble since he got here," the man continued, "and this is just the latest example!"

"But—Brian's not responsible for the situation he's in now," Mr. Clark said, sounding confused.

"I don't care!" a woman said, also standing up. "I don't want my kids hanging around somebody who's from a destructive home."

"People, please—I haven't finished my announcement yet." Mr. Clark looked uneasily around at the noisy crowd. "I realize that this is an extremely emotional issue. And the state realizes that as well. I'm sorry to say that they have decided to place the student away from his parents, in another school district."

Several parents in the audience applauded.

Mr. Clark held up his hands. "Please, everyone. Our job here as parents and teachers is to figure out what's best for our students. And for this student, I strongly feel it would be in his best interest to *remain* at this school, where people know him and can help him—"

"And hate him," Maria muttered.

Elizabeth stared at her friend. How could Maria hate somebody who had already suffered through so much?

"And that's why I've called this meeting. Now, with the support of this community, I believe we can petition the state to let Brian stay at Sweet Valley Middle School, and find a foster family for him in our town. This would be an unusual procedure, but it has been done before," Mr. Clark said.

Elizabeth felt a surge of hope and gratitude. Mr.

Clark wanted to help Brian as much as she did! She listened carefully as he went on, anxious to find out how she could help with the petition.

"I feel that the student has had enough problems and upheaval in his life lately. The last thing he needs is to be shipped to a new school. So, with a show of hands, could I see how many people support this idea? Who will sign the petition to keep Brian at our school?" Mr. Clark smiled, scanning the crowd for supporters.

Elizabeth raised her hand. Mrs. Sutton, Amy's mother, also voted to sign the petition. Maria's parents didn't raise their hands. As Elizabeth expected, Maria didn't, either.

Elizabeth looked around the audience. Only half the people wanted Brian to stay. She drew in her breath. They probably wouldn't have enough signatures for the petition.

"Keep your hands up just another minute, until I count everyone," Mr. Clark requested.

However many you count, it won't be enough, Elizabeth thought. She glanced at her parents, hoping to share an understanding look. But what she saw almost made her do a double take.

Her mother wasn't voting to keep Brian at Sweet Valley Middle School—and neither was her father!

Elizabeth couldn't believe it. What about all those things they'd said, about Brian needing help and making sure he got what he needed? What about her mother telling Jessica they should all stick together? They weren't standing up for Brian; they didn't care enough to help him. Nobody did!

Her father caught her staring at him, and he smiled uneasily at her, shifting in his chair. Elizabeth frowned. If her own parents weren't going to support Brian . . . who was?

"I don't know why Mr. Clark's bothering to count. It's obvious that he doesn't have enough votes," Maria commented as she jotted down a figure in her notebook.

Elizabeth stared at her as she calmly wrote. "Maria, do you *really* want Brian to leave our school?"

She nodded. "Sure."

"But—he needs to have friends around. He just lost his whole family," Elizabeth argued.

Maria shrugged. "So? It doesn't sound like any big loss, the way they acted."

Elizabeth felt her face heat up. Something told her that it hurt whenever somebody lost their family, no matter why or how. All of a sudden she couldn't bear to stay at the meeting a second longer with everyone else so against helping Brian. "I—I have to go," she told Maria hurriedly.

Elizabeth stood up and felt her legs trembling as she hurried out of the auditorium. She didn't want to wait around for her parents. As far as she was concerned, they'd betrayed her—and Brian, too. She didn't want to talk to them tonight, or anytime soon. How could they be so heartless?

Nine

◇

Ten minutes later, Elizabeth was riding her bike down the street by the Boyds' house when she spotted a figure at the fence surrounding their property. At first her breath caught in her throat. What if it was Mr. Boyd? Then her eyes adjusted to the light, and she saw that it was Brian.

She heaved a sigh of relief. Without even thinking about it, she coasted to a stop in front of him. "Hi," she said nervously.

"Hey," he said. "How's it going?"

"OK," Elizabeth said, a little surprised that he was talking to her. She got off her bike and leaned it against the fence. "How are you?"

"Cool." Brian nodded. "I know I shouldn't be here, but . . ." He shrugged. "I kind of miss the old neighborhood, you know?"

"Yeah." *He probably misses his parents,* Elizabeth realized. *No matter what happened, they're still his parents.*

"So where are you living now?" she asked. Then she wanted to take it back—she already knew that he didn't have a permanent place to stay yet. "I'm sorry. I'm not trying to pry," she quickly added. "You don't have to tell me anything."

"No, it's OK," Brian said. He gazed over at his old house. None of the lights were on inside, and it looked dark and foreboding. "I have this new foster family." He turned back around to face Elizabeth. "They're great. The dad's the president of a bank, and the mom is like some hotshot tax attorney. Totally cool people."

Elizabeth nodded, unsure what to say next. She knew Brian was lying about having a new home. But she wasn't about to tell him that she knew. He probably needed to lie. He obviously didn't want her to know just how bad his situation was.

And she wouldn't tell him something else she knew: that things were actually going to get worse.

"So, did you write that dumb essay for Bowman yet?" Brian asked.

Elizabeth shrugged. "Yeah. But I'm not happy with it. I mean, what I wrote sounds really stupid. Really, incredibly stupid." *And untrue. I thought my parents were the kindest people in the whole world when I wrote it. I know differently now.*

"Yeah," Brian sighed. "Mine's dumb, too." He

hopped off the fence and landed on his feet beside Elizabeth. "Well, I should get going. I'm supposed to be back at the cen—I mean, back home—by eight."

"Yeah, I should go, too," Elizabeth said. "So . . . See you tomorrow."

"Right. Tomorrow. Man, I can't believe it's only Tuesday. This has got to be the longest week in history." He picked up his mountain bike, climbed on and rode away, leaving Elizabeth standing there under a tree, in the dark.

"The longest week in history," she murmured. "Not to mention the worst."

Brian didn't know it yet, but tomorrow might be his last day at Sweet Valley Middle School. And there was nothing Elizabeth or anyone else could do about it, even if they tried.

"Honey?" There was a knock on Elizabeth's door. She didn't answer. She didn't want to talk to either one of her parents.

"Elizabeth, can we talk to you for a second?" her father asked.

"Please?" her mother added in a desperate tone.

Elizabeth shook her head and got up from her desk. If she didn't let them in, they'd stand there knocking all night. She opened the door and stared at both of them, arms folded across her chest. "What do you want?"

They both looked taken aback. "Just—to talk to you.

About what happened tonight," Mrs. Wakefield said.

"What's there to talk about?" Elizabeth asked.

"Well, you . . . ran out of the meeting so quickly," her father said. "We were worried. Are you . . . all right?"

"Yes, I'm fine," Elizabeth said in a clipped tone. "Too bad Brian isn't, but I guess he can just deal with that when he finds out he's being carted off to some other town."

Mrs. Wakefield frowned. "Elizabeth, are you angry with us because we voted differently from you?"

"You could say that." Elizabeth threw up her hands. "Look, what's the point of saying you'll help Brian, and then sending him to another town?"

"We didn't send him anywhere," Mr. Wakefield protested. "The state did."

"Maybe so, but you didn't try to stop them. That makes you just as guilty," Elizabeth responded. "Now if you don't mind, I have a lot of work to do."

"Elizabeth, don't be mad at us—we're only trying to do the right thing for everyone!" Mrs. Wakefield pleaded.

Instead of responding, Elizabeth shut the door. She leaned against it, her heart beating quickly. She had never argued with her parents like that. But then again, she'd never thought they were really wrong about something before.

The right thing for everyone? What about the right thing for Brian?

*   *   *

"Mr. Bowman?" Elizabeth stopped by her teacher's desk on Wednesday morning after English.

"Yes, Elizabeth?" Mr. Bowman smiled at her.

"I know Brian wasn't in class today, and I was just wondering if you knew whether he was in school at all," Elizabeth said. "I'm not trying to be nosy or anything—it's just that . . . I owe him some money and I wanted to give it back." She didn't want to tell Mr. Bowman why she was really looking for him.

"Hmm. Well, actually, Elizabeth, I don't know where Brian is," Mr. Bowman said.

"You don't?"

Mr. Bowman shook his head. "I haven't heard anything."

"Well . . . do you know who might know?" Elizabeth asked. "I really want to—I mean, he might need the money or whatever."

"I'm sorry—I can't help you, Elizabeth. I don't think anyone knows where he is today," Mr. Bowman said. "Unless Mr. Clark does, but he hasn't said anything to me."

"Brian wouldn't just be . . . gone, would he?" Elizabeth asked.

Mr. Bowman set a file folder down on his desk. "You were at the PTA meeting last night, weren't you? I forgot—you're one of the student representatives."

Elizabeth nodded. "Were you there, too? I didn't see you."

"I wasn't going to go because I already had other plans, and it was so last-minute," Mr. Bowman said. "But when I heard it was going to be about Brian, I had to be there. Even though he isn't always the easiest student to deal with, I do care about him. The same way I care about all of my students."

"I figured," Elizabeth said. "I just feel like all everyone wants to do is forget about Brian—make him move to some other state, some other country, just so they don't have to deal with him!"

Mr. Bowman nodded. "Yes. People are very afraid, I guess."

"But *I'm* afraid, too, Mr. Bowman," Elizabeth said. "Only it doesn't make me want to run away, it makes me want to help. Because if nobody steps in and helps Brian now . . . well, who knows what will happen to him."

"I agree," Mr. Bowman said. "Don't worry, Elizabeth. We'll think of something. It'll turn out OK."

Elizabeth smiled faintly at Mr. Bowman. *I hope you're right.*

"OK, everyone. Class is ending fifteen minutes early today, and we're all heading to the auditorium for a special assembly with Mr. Clark," Mrs. Arnette announced in Elizabeth's social studies class that afternoon. "Get your things together quickly now."

Elizabeth stuffed her notebook into her backpack.

"What do you think this is about?" Amy asked, falling into step beside Elizabeth as they walked out of the classroom and down the hall.

Elizabeth shrugged. "I don't know, but it seems kind of weird, doesn't it?"

Amy nodded. "Maybe it has something to do with the PTA meeting last night. My mother said it was really intense."

"Yeah, I was there," Elizabeth said. "And you wouldn't believe what happened."

"She told me how Mr. Clark asked everyone to help sign a petition to keep Brian here, and that less than half the people would," Amy said. "That's so pathetic. Why do people want him to leave so much?"

"Why should he be allowed to stay?" Maria asked, coming up behind the two girls. "School was better before he came here, and it'll be better when he leaves."

Elizabeth glanced at Maria and frowned. "Listen, Maria, if you had seen Brian like I saw him—," she began, then stopped herself. She couldn't tell Maria about how Brian had been crying or about how lonely he was. She knew Brian wouldn't want anyone else to know. "Never mind," she told Maria.

The three girls walked into the auditorium with the steady stream of students taking seats. Once everyone was seated, Mr. Clark walked onto the stage with a woman Elizabeth didn't recognize.

"Good afternoon, everyone." Mr. Clark rubbed

his forehead and looked out at the audience. "Thanks for coming. We don't have much time, so I'd like to get down to business right away."

Elizabeth fidgeted nervously in her seat. Mr. Clark sounded so serious. And who was that woman with him? A horrible thought came to her: What if Brian wasn't in school because something had happened to him? What if his parents . . . took him back? Kidnapped him?

"As many of you know, we've had a lot of rumors around school recently concerning child abuse," Mr. Clark said. "A lot of different stories have been going around concerning one individual. And while it's unfortunate that a student here is in this situation, what is equally unfortunate is the way that some people have been blaming this person for his misfortune. I want you all to understand that when child abuse occurs, the child has nothing whatsoever to do with it. In no circumstances is it acceptable to hold a child responsible for his or her parents' actions," Mr. Clark said sternly.

"Now, to help you understand further, I've invited a psychologist, Dr. Pam Delgaty, to explain a few things. She's an expert in this field, and I hope you'll take what she says to heart. Dr. Delgaty?" Mr. Clark stepped away from the microphone.

So they *were* taking Brian's situation seriously, Elizabeth thought, sitting up a little straighter in her seat. Things weren't as bad as she thought! If

Mr. Clark wanted to make sure everyone understood, that could only mean Brian would be sticking around Sweet Valley. Maybe Mr. Clark's petition had worked!

The doctor stepped over to the podium. "Thank you, Mr. Clark." She gazed out at all of the assembled students. "And thank you all for listening. I won't keep you long, but I just want to impress upon you a few vital facts about child abuse. One, as Mr. Clark said, a child has no control over what happens to him or her. When parents are mean to their children, either by becoming violent or by saying angry things, the children have absolutely nothing to do with it. It's not because they're bad kids, or because they did something wrong, or said something they shouldn't have."

She should have spoken to the parents here last night! Elizabeth thought.

"Now, when children are mistreated that way by their parents," Dr. Delgaty went on, "they can react in several different ways. With some kids, you'd never know anything bad was happening at home. They act completely normal on the outside, but they're hurting inside. They may hide this problem deep inside for months, or years, in the belief that it will go away by itself. Or they may become very quiet and withdrawn because they believe they really are at fault. They may keep trying to behave better and better—when in reality, it doesn't matter *how* they behave. If their parents are going to mistreat them, they are. The kids can't stop them."

"This is so scary," Amy whispered to Elizabeth. She nodded. "It must be awful to go through this."

"Another possible reaction," Dr. Delgaty continued, "is that the abused child will act out what's happening to him on other people. In other words, he will copy the behavior of his parents, in part because that's all he knows, in part to deal with his feelings of anger and low self-worth."

Brian, Elizabeth thought.

"The good news is, all of these children suffering from child abuse can be helped. But before we can help them, we must try to understand them. They love their parents, and their parents have betrayed their trust. It might be difficult, but try to imagine how awful you would feel if you could no longer trust or rely on your parents. That's how abused children feel. Understanding this takes patience, and it takes a lot of love. Thank you all for listening." Dr. Delgaty smiled and stepped away from the microphone.

"Wow," Elizabeth said. "She was good."

Amy nodded. "I'd kind of heard all that stuff before, but it still helps to have it explained."

Elizabeth glanced at Maria. She was staring straight ahead, a puzzled expression on her face. "Maria?" Elizabeth asked softly. "Are you OK?"

Maria glanced at Elizabeth. "Oh. Yeah. Sure."

Elizabeth wondered if the reality of Brian's situation was finally starting to hit her friend. But she didn't have time to ask, because just then Mr. Clark stepped behind the podium on stage.

"I hope that helped." Mr. Clark dabbed at his forehead with a handkerchief. He seemed extremely nervous. "Now a few quick announcements, and then I'll let you go." He cleared his throat. "First, you might have noticed that repair work is being done on the south wing. It should be finished in a few days. Second, the pep rally originally scheduled for this afternoon has been postponed until next week. And third, Brian Boyd has been transferred to Big Mesa Middle School." He looked at the crowd and nodded. "That will be all." Then Mr. Clark practically ran off the stage, disappearing behind the stage curtain.

Elizabeth sat quietly, too stunned to move. Brian was moving after all . . . to Big Mesa? But—what about all the things Dr. Delgaty had just said, about patience, love, and understanding?

"Why are they doing this to him?" she asked, her voice breaking, as everyone around her stood and started to gather their things. "This is so wrong!"

"Why is it wrong?" Maria asked. "I mean, if that's where the foster family is—"

"But don't you get it? He doesn't *have* to move," Elizabeth argued. "Mr. Clark said a precedent's been set for keeping a student from being transferred just because he moves. We can all sign a petition and Brian can stay. Only people won't sign it, because they just want him to move away so they don't have to deal with this!"

"Well, I don't want to deal with it, either," Maria said. "It's Brian's problem, anyway."

"No, it's not," Elizabeth said. "It's *everyone's* problem. And if we don't do something to help Brian, then we're turning our backs on every kid out there who's being abused."

"But, Elizabeth, he'll get help! Just not in Sweet Valley," Maria protested.

Elizabeth's temper flared. "Is that fair? Why should he have to leave behind everyone he knows because of something that isn't his fault? Didn't you *hear* any of what that doctor just said?"

"I heard her!" Maria said, just as passionately. Her eyes filled with tears. "It's just . . . Elizabeth, what could we do, anyway?"

"I don't know, Maria." Elizabeth looked into Maria's eyes and felt a tear trickle down her own cheek. "But if this town doesn't do something to help kids in trouble—if Sweet Valley actually makes their lives even harder—then I'm not sure I even want to live here anymore!"

Ten

"I have a plan," Jessica announced as she and Lila walked home from school Wednesday afternoon.

Lila's face lit up. "Are you sneaking out tomorrow night—to come to the party?"

"No," Jessica sighed. *She would have to remind me that I'm missing the party of the year.*

"I can't believe you're going to miss Snob Hill Night," Lila said. "It's, like . . . unheard of."

"Yeah, well. I told you, my parents are impossible," Jessica said bitterly. "Anyway, you know how I've been putting all this information together for our essay for Mr. Bowman's class?"

"You mean the one that was due today? What, did Mr. Bowman give you an extension?" Lila asked.

"Until tomorrow. I'm almost done," Jessica said. *It's all in my head, anyway. And on all those scrap pieces of napkin lying around my desk.* "You know how my parents have been acting so strict, and how they keep doing all these parenting things wrong."

"Well, that's what *you* say," Lila interrupted.

Jessica raised one eyebrow. "Do you think I don't know what I'm doing? I've even read every handout Mr. Bowman's given us, plus the textbook. And according to my calculations, my parents need some serious reorganizing of their parental skills."

"So what's your plan?" Lila asked.

"I've decided to give them one final, all-or-nothing test," Jessica said excitedly. "If they pass it—no problem. I can confidently report in my essay to the class that they are the best parents ever. And if they don't . . . well, I'll be forced to tell everyone just how thoughtless they really are when it comes to their daughter."

"What kind of test?" Lila asked.

"I'm going to see if they trust me enough to promise me my own car when I turn sixteen," Jessica announced proudly.

Lila laughed. "Jessica, I thought you were serious about this."

"I am!" Jessica cried.

"Come on, even I'm not that superficial," Lila said. "What does giving you a car have to do with anything?"

"You're the one who said that your dad's great because he gives you what you want," Jessica reminded her.

"Yeah, but if he only did that, he wouldn't be a good parent," Lila said. "Money's not everything, you know."

Jessica remembered saying the same thing at the mall last week, about Brian. She pictured his face. He looked so sad the last time she saw him. She pushed the thought away. He was leaving Sweet Valley, and that was that.

"My dad's a good parent because he looks out for me, he takes care of me, and, you know, because he treats me well," Lila went on.

Jessica looked at Lila. "And that's all I'm asking—to be treated the same way you are. With my own car!"

Lila just shook her head and kept walking.

Jessica kicked a rock with her sandal and followed Lila slowly down the street. Some people just didn't understand. Sure it was easy for Lila to call Jessica superficial—Lila always got what she wanted!

Elizabeth knocked gently on her sister's door Wednesday night. "Jessica, are you busy?"

"You can come in," Jessica said.

Elizabeth walked into her sister's room, carefully stepping over piles of discarded outfits and old fashion magazines. Her sister was constantly cleaning her room, then constantly getting it messy again. "Hi." She perched on the edge of Jessica's bed.

Jessica turned around from her desk. "What's up?"

"I just don't feel like doing any homework," Elizabeth said.

"Neither do I." Jessica pointed at a bottle of pink fingernail polish on her desk and giggled. "I'm supposed to be working on my essay, but I was actually about to do my nails. Talk about procrastinating."

"Yeah. Pretty bad." Elizabeth took a deep breath. The only way to talk about this was to just plunge in, before she lost her nerve. "I know you're going to think I'm crazy, but I really need to talk to someone, and I can't talk to Mom and Dad. They don't understand." In fact, she'd barely said two words to her parents since the night before. She couldn't forgive them—or understand, either. "Anyway, it's about Brian. I just can't get him out of my head," she admitted to Jessica.

Jessica looked at her as if she had lost her mind. "You mean . . . Brian Boyd?"

Elizabeth frowned. "Yes, of course Brian Boyd!"

"Oh," Jessica said. "Well, what about him?"

"Jessica, come on. You haven't said one word about Brian since this whole thing came up," Elizabeth said. "How do you feel? Isn't it bothering you?"

"Are you training to be a psychologist or something?" Jessica asked, wrinkling her nose.

"No, of course not." Elizabeth sighed with exasperation. "Look, I'm sorry if I sounded formal. It's just that it's so upsetting."

"I guess," Jessica said.

"You guess?" Elizabeth repeated.

"What are you getting at?" Jessica asked.

"Look, I came in here because I wanted to ask for your help," Elizabeth said, standing up. "I wanted to see if you'd help me think of a way to keep Brian from moving away. But I can see you're too busy painting your nails to actually help anyone besides yourself, so I'll go."

"Wait a second," Jessica said, also standing up abruptly. Her desk chair clattered to the floor. "I didn't say I didn't care what happened! I just don't know how I'm supposed to help. You tell me what I'm supposed to do since you have all the answers."

"One thing you could do is stop gossiping about him," Elizabeth said.

"I *haven't* gossiped about him!" Jessica cried.

Elizabeth folded her arms. She had been trying not to think of Jessica's breaking her promise and blowing Brian's secret. But seeing how unconcerned Jessica was, she couldn't help feeling furious. "Oh, come on. We both know that you're the one who started the rumors about Brian in the first place, after I swore you to secrecy. And because of that, you're partly responsible for everyone being so against Brian, because people got the wrong information."

"I am not responsible for that!" Jessica argued. "I told Lila and Janet the truth, but they didn't understand me—"

"No wonder," Elizabeth said. "Because I don't understand you either!"

"Look, Elizabeth, a lot of people knew about it, and I didn't tell all of those people," Jessica insisted. "What do you think, that I like to make people unhappy? Anyway, what am I supposed to do about it now? Brian's moved away. End of story!"

"Fine. You want to stick your head in the sand and pretend this never happened?" Elizabeth asked. "Go ahead. But I can't. The next time you have a problem, remind me to ignore you, then you'll see how it feels." She walked out of the room, slamming the door behind her.

Jessica glanced at the neatly typed essay on her desk Thursday morning. She'd done an excellent job, if she did say so herself. It was nice of Mr. Bowman to have given her the extension; all he'd asked was that she read her essay out loud this morning, just like everyone else, and he wouldn't even mark her down for handing it in late.

Even the title of her essay went straight to the point: "Parenting Made Easy," by Jessica Wakefield. In her essay, she'd listed common errors parents made and possible ways to correct them. Her research wasn't quite complete: She hadn't gotten an answer from her parents about the car issue yet. But she'd simply added a blank page at the end of her essay marked "Epilogue: The Final Story."

Everyone thinks Elizabeth is the literary one in the family. Ha! Wait till they hear this. I might even start writing for the Sixers; *they could use a good investigative reporter.*

She glanced up as her sister walked into the classroom. They'd barely exchanged two words since their argument the night before. Jessica knit her brow as she thought about what Elizabeth had said. Who was Elizabeth to tell her she didn't care about Brian? She cared. She just knew when to give up on lost causes.

I mean, if I could help Brian, I would, she told herself. But it was obvious the matter was out of her hands. Practically everyone thought Brian should transfer to another school.

"I've had a chance to read all of your essays," Mr. Bowman announced when everyone was in their seats. "And I'm happy to say that there were several excellent ones. Several." He walked around the room, handing back everyone's papers.

Jessica sneaked a glance over at Elizabeth. Normally her twin's face lit up when she got an essay back. But she just shoved it into her notebook and looked up at Mr. Bowman.

How could Elizabeth do badly on an essay? Jessica wondered. *And if she did, then what does that say about my chances of winning?*

"I was going to ask all of you to read your essays this morning," Mr. Bowman said, "since you all worked hard and since not everyone can read theirs at Saturday's ceremony. However, I've changed my mind."

Jessica raised her hand. "You're still going to accept mine, right?"

"Oh, of course, Jessica," Mr. Bowman said. "But I thought that we might spend today thinking about one essay in particular. It really had quite an effect on me last night. I thought you might want to hear it, too."

Jessica scanned the room anxiously. Whose essay was it? Who hadn't gotten theirs back? Or was he going to read Elizabeth's, after all?

"The author will remain anonymous," Mr. Bowman said, taking a sheet of paper out of his briefcase.

It's only one page, Jessica thought with a satisfied smirk. *How good can it be?*

Mr. Bowman cleared his throat and started reading.

"'Once upon a time, there was a family that lived in a big city. The father was a very successful businessman, and the mother acted and modeled part-time. They had a son whom they loved very much. Everything was perfect.

"'If you believe that real families are anything like the ones in the fairy tales you read when you were young, you're wrong. Parents might start out being kings and queens to their children, but they don't always stay that way. No one can say exactly why, or what happens. All we know is that one day, the children live in a castle, and the next day, it's a dungeon. And nobody says why. And everybody acts like it's your fault.

"'But you didn't do anything. You just woke up one day and your parents weren't there anymore. Instead of the good, kind queen, there's a wicked one. The king's throne has been taken over by someone else.

"'What can you do? You're only a kid. You could run away, but where would you go? You could tell someone, but who would listen?

"'So you sit in your room and you hope. You hope that things will change. You hope that your mother and father will come back someday. That those other people who look like them and talk like them will leave you alone until then.

"'But you can't keep hoping forever. Because hope is something that you run out of. And once it's gone, it may never return. Like your parents.'"

Mr. Bowman slowly lowered the paper, his voice trembling at the end.

Jessica felt a tear trickle down her cheek. That was Brian's essay. She'd never imagined how truly, absolutely awful and alone he must feel.

And here she'd been getting upset when she didn't get her favorite meal, complaining about not being allowed to go to a sleepover, and asking for extra *money*. She'd been so blind. She was the lucky one. Her parents were wonderful to her. And Brian was the one who needed things he didn't get. Like love.

She picked the essay off her desk and crumpled all four pages into a ball.

*   *   *

Even after Mr. Bowman had stopped reading, Elizabeth couldn't make herself look up at him. Her eyes were filled with tears. Finally she sneaked a glance around the room. Nobody was talking or moving, although she saw Jessica crumpling up some papers on her desk. Everyone looked completely devastated.

And suddenly she knew what she had to do.

Elizabeth raised her hand. "Mr. Bowman?" she asked, her voice shaky. "Would it be OK if I made an announcement?"

"Of course," Mr. Bowman said. "The floor is yours."

Elizabeth stood up, balancing herself by putting her hand on the desk. "I don't know how everyone feels about Brian Boyd being sent to another school, but I don't think it's fair for him to be sent away for something that's not his fault. I want him to stay at Sweet Valley Middle School. If our parents won't help, maybe we can. So I'm asking everyone who wants to help to come to a meeting this afternoon. Maybe together we can think of a way to help Brian."

For a second, nobody moved.

Then a chair on the other side of the room scraped against the floor. "I'll be there," Jessica said. She glanced shyly at Elizabeth.

I knew she'd come through for me, Elizabeth thought, giving her sister a tentative smile.

"Me, too," Amy said.

"Count me in," Todd added.

Maria looked up at Elizabeth. "What time should we be there? And where will it be?"

She smiled at Maria. "Two-thirty. How about the gym?"

"Well, you'd need a member of the faculty with you in order to use the gym for a meeting," Mr. Bowman pointed out.

"Oh," Elizabeth said, her heart sinking.

"So I'll be there, too," he said, putting Brian's essay back into his briefcase. "Now, Jessica—you wanted to turn your essay in today?"

She shook her head. "I just realized I have to rewrite it. I made some major mistakes."

"Some typos?"

"Not exactly," Jessica said, smiling at Elizabeth. "I have to rewrite it to include some things I learned today."

Eleven

◇

"Welcome to the First Annual Family Reception!" Mr. Bowman cheerfully announced to the huge audience of parents Saturday morning. "We're so glad you could all come down to visit with us and learn a little about what we've been discussing for the past two weeks."

Elizabeth tapped her feet in anticipation. She'd hardly slept the night before, she was so anxious about the reception. Her meeting with almost ninety percent of her classmates Thursday afternoon had gone very well—even better than she'd expected. Now all they had to do was put their plan into action.

The cafeteria was dressed up with streamers and balloons. Plates of home-baked cookies and brownies covered one table. It looked just like any other Sweet Valley Middle School party—except for all the parents standing and sitting around. *And except for what we've planned,* Elizabeth thought. She crossed her fingers behind her back for luck.

"We'd like to get started this morning with a little overview of what we've all been studying for the past two weeks," Mr. Bowman said. "In case you thought your son or daughter was crazy, following you around the kitchen with that microphone, taking down your every word—"

The room filled with laughter.

"Well, he or she was actually doing an assignment. We've all been talking about what makes families work, what it's like to be a parent, and a child. And as many of you know, we held a contest for the best essay on that subject," Mr. Bowman said. "But we have something we want to read to you instead, and here to read it is Elizabeth Wakefield." He stepped away from the podium and gestured for Elizabeth to take his place.

She stood up and walked over to him. "Go get 'em," he whispered in her ear.

Elizabeth nodded and stepped up to the podium. "Hi," she said, feeling a little unsure of herself. She'd spoken in public many times before, and she normally didn't get so nervous. But there usually wasn't so much at stake.

"Mr. Bowman asked me a few days ago if I would read my essay today, and I agreed,"

Elizabeth said. "But then something happened. I found something better—it's a letter."

She heard murmurs in the crowd, and she looked around the cafeteria for a familiar face. Jessica gave her the thumbs-up signal, and Elizabeth smiled.

"It's something that we all wrote. Everyone of us in this room. And we want you all to hear it and to listen to what we're saying." She cleared her throat and, hands shaking, put the essay on the podium.

"'Dear Parents,'" Elizabeth read. "'We got together to write this letter as a group, because we believe that there is power in numbers. Something happened recently that has affected us all. We respect your authority and trust your judgment, but in this particular case we think you made the wrong decision.'" Elizabeth paused for a moment before continuing. She could hear a few parents murmuring to each other.

"'We don't think that transferring Brian Boyd to another school is the best way to handle his problems,'" Elizabeth continued. "'And we're disappointed that you wouldn't sign the petition Mr. Clark offered as a way to keep Brian in our community. We feel that you didn't sign the petition because you were glad to see Brian go, as if he would take all of the problems away with him. As we've learned from Mr. Clark and others, child abuse is not the fault of the child. Punishing Brian by removing him from school is like blaming him for something he didn't do, and that's wrong.'"

Elizabeth took a deep breath and glanced up at her audience. It seemed as though thousands of eyes were staring at her intently. "'Transferring Brian to Big Mesa won't make child abuse go away. What's worse, it might discourage another kid from seeking help if he's in the same situation, because he or she wouldn't want to be sent away, either. What kind of a community are we to turn our backs on people with problems?'"

"'What we would like is for all of our parents to take responsibility for Brian. Mr. Bowman taught us once that when you become a parent, you're not only responsible for your own child, but for children everywhere,'" Elizabeth said carefully. "'We all strongly believe that while you have succeeded in your first job . . . you have failed in your second. Please, give Brian another chance. He needs you. He needs all of us. Sincerely, Your Children.'" Elizabeth looked up at the crowd. "That's all we have to say. Thanks for listening."

She started to walk back to her table. She could hear the click of her heels on the linoleum floor. The room was completely silent, as if everyone was too stunned to speak. She glanced at her parents as she took her seat, and they were both staring at her with confused expressions on their faces.

Then Elizabeth's father stood up and cleared his throat. "How about if all the parents go into the auditorium to discuss our reply to your letter?"

Mr. Clark nodded. "I'll come along, if that's all right." Elizabeth watched as all of the parents filed out of the cafeteria, talking as they went. "Do you think our letter worked?" she asked Maria anxiously.

Maria shrugged. "I can't tell. I guess we'll just have to wait."

Elizabeth sank into her chair. "That's what I was afraid of."

"Look at it this way, Elizabeth—if it doesn't work out, at least we tried our best," Amy said.

Elizabeth nodded. She knew Amy was right, but deep down, she felt that just trying didn't count—not this time.

Elizabeth watched as her father and mother re-entered the cafeteria. It seemed as if they had been in the auditorium an hour. But it had actually only been ten minutes, she noticed, glancing at the clock.

Her father walked slowly up to the podium, holding a piece of paper. The room fell silent as all the students around Elizabeth stopped their conversations midsentence to listen.

Mr. Wakefield looked around the cafeteria at the crowd. "Well, I've been appointed spokesperson for the parents, so here goes," he said, nervously rolling up his shirtsleeves. "'Dear Kids. We got together and talked about what you all presented to us here today. And while we all agreed that you made some very good points . . .'"

Uh-oh, Elizabeth thought. *This doesn't sound good.*

"'. . . we wanted you to know why we acted the way we did,'" her father continued, "'so you can understand that though it may seem we acted uncharitably at times, our main concern has *always* been being good parents.

"'What we want to say today, as a group, is that we owe you all an apology. We reacted out of panic. We made a bad decision because of our desire to protect you, and we're sorry.'" He looked at Elizabeth. "'It's also our job as parents to try and teach our children right from wrong. But sometimes we fail, and it's our kids who end up teaching us instead.'"

As he paused to turn over the sheet of paper, Elizabeth felt her heart beating hard. "'After careful consideration,'" Mr. Wakefield continued, "'we've decided to sign Mr. Clark's petition, urging the state to reconsider their decision. We'll ask them to place Brian in a foster home right here in Sweet Valley. That way he can stay in this school. And as long as he's willing to seek help for his problems, we will help him as much as we can.'"

"Yes!" Elizabeth shrieked, jumping out of her chair as the whole room erupted into cheers. She ran straight across the room to her father and threw herself into his arms. Then Elizabeth hugged her mother as kids all around her celebrated with their parents.

"Thanks for understanding," Elizabeth told her parents.

"Sorry it took us so long," Mr. Wakefield said sheepishly.

"We were just worried about you," Mrs. Wakefield added. "Those nightmares, and the way you were so distracted, and—"

"I know," Elizabeth said. "But the person we all needed to worry about was Brian." She saw Mr. Clark coming toward the podium. Before he could say anything, she ran up to him and hugged him tightly.

"Well, uh, Elizabeth." His face turned bright pink. "I'm glad everything worked out, too. But if you'll let me go, I have something else to say."

"Oh." Elizabeth giggled, releasing her hold on Mr. Clark. "Sorry."

"No problem," Mr. Clark said. He stepped up to the podium at the center of the cafeteria. "Now, Brian hasn't been moved to Big Mesa yet. The foster parents there weren't quite ready for him, because they were waiting for their current foster child to move into his new adoptive home. So Brian's still in a temporary shelter. The question now is, can we find a foster family in town for him?" Mr. Clark looked around at the crowd. "Does anyone know of someone who could take Brian in?"

"I'll ask around," Mrs. Sutton said.

"If we spread the word, I bet we can have someone by tonight," Mr. Slater suggested.

"Remember—a foster home has to be one that's officially approved and certified by the state," Mr. Clark said. "It can't just be somebody who's willing

to help. Kids in foster homes need special care—
parents who have special training."

Elizabeth smiled at Mr. Clark. Why hadn't she
thought of it before? Mr. and Mrs. Hubler, who
lived a few streets down from the Wakefields, were
foster parents. They'd had kids stay with them for
two weeks, or two years . . . they were always taking in people who had nowhere else to go. She
could at least mention the Hublers to Mr. Clark and
ask him to have the state check into it.

So maybe she wasn't helpless, after all.

"Mr. Clark?" she said, walking over to him. "I
think I might know someone who could take Brian."

"That's great!" Mr. Clark said. "Boy, that was some
group effort you put together. Was that your idea?"

Elizabeth shrugged. "I think I just acted on what
everyone else was feeling. At first we were all so
afraid that none of us could take action. You know
what I mean?"

Mr. Clark nodded. "I've been there, believe me.
You don't think I ever wanted Brian to leave,
though, do you? I mean, maybe the time he put salt
in the sugar dispenser in the teachers' lounge . . . or
the time he—well, never mind. That's the past.
We'll have to work on his future."

Elizabeth smiled. With the Sweet Valley community supporting him, Brian had a shot at a good future now.

Twelve

"Mom? Dad?" Jessica stood in the doorway of the living room Saturday afternoon, looking anxiously at her parents. She was so choked up, she could barely talk.

"Are you here for the answer to your quiz?" her father asked with a grin as he put down the book he'd been reading.

"Quiz?" Jessica asked.

"About getting a car when you turn sixteen," Mr. Wakefield reminded her.

"Oh. That." Jessica shook her head, a little embarrassed. "No. I'm here—I'm here because . . ." The words caught in her throat. "I want to—I have to apologize. About everything!" She burst into tears and ran straight to her parents, who were sitting on the couch. She fell to the floor and buried her face in the cushions. "I'm so sorry!" she said, her voice muffled by the fabric.

"Oh, Jessica. It's OK, honey," her mother said, stroking Jessica's hair.

"I've been so awful," Jessica said through sobs. "Hounding you about every little thing and making all those stupid demands and—"

Mr. Wakefield gently lifted Jessica by the shoulders. "Honey, we can't hear you when you talk into the sofa. Unless, of course, you're apologizing to the sofa?"

Jessica couldn't help smiling. She brushed the tears off her cheeks and sat down between her parents. "I'm sorry. I just feel like such a creep after everything I've been asking you for. More money, more clothes, going to that stupid sleepover. I won't need to ask you guys for anything ever again!"

"You won't?" Mrs. Wakefield looked suspicious.

"No, I won't," Jessica said.

"Well, you might need to eat sometimes," Mr. Wakefield said smiling.

"I'm serious!" Jessica insisted. "I didn't need any of those things I was asking for . . . not really. Because you guys are great parents. You give me everything that really counts. Like . . . love, and patience, and understanding." She started crying again. "All the things Brian's parents stopped giving him."

Her mother wrapped her arms around Jessica's shoulders and squeezed her tightly. "It's OK. Brian's going to be OK."

Jessica nodded, sniffling. "I hope so."

"How do you feel about what's been happening?" Mr. Wakefield asked. "You haven't said anything about it, so I wondered."

"I just kept trying not to think about it," Jessica confessed. "At first when I found out, it seemed so horrible. It *is* so horrible. So then I guess I just pushed it out of my mind, because . . . I don't know. It was scary."

"That's not so unusual," her mother said. "I mean, you handled it the only way you knew how. But maybe next time you should feel you can talk about something that's bothering you . . . instead of trying to bury it all inside. We'll always be willing to listen."

Jessica nodded. "Yeah, I know. Oh, hey—there's something I wanted you to see." She pulled out a crumpled, tearstained piece of paper from her pocket. "Uh-oh. Looks like I'll have to print a new copy of this for Mr. Bowman. But you guys can have this one."

Her father took the slightly damp, mushed paper. "Gee . . . umm, thanks, I guess."

"You're supposed to read it, silly," Jessica said with a laugh.

"I don't know if I can." He strained to make out the blurred words.

"OK, I'll print you a new copy, too," Jessica said, hopping off the couch. "But just so you know, I threw out my old essay and wrote a whole new one last night. I think I know a little more about the whole parenting thing now."

"Really," her father teased. "Do you have any pointers?"

Jessica shrugged. "Well, I'm now an expert on parenting, so if I can help . . ."

"We'll be sure to let you know if we need advice," Mrs. Wakefield told her, smiling wryly.

Jessica giggled. "Hey, I know this doesn't matter anymore, but I was just wondering. About that quiz? What was your answer going to be, anyway?"

"About getting your own car?" Mrs. Wakefield asked.

Jessica nodded eagerly.

"Well, we did give it some very serious consideration, of course," her father said. "We weighed the pros, the cons. We read the articles. We looked at auto magazines. We checked out car prices—"

"You did!" Jessica shrieked.

Mr. Wakefield nodded. "And we definitely made a decision."

"Well? What is it?" she demanded.

"You just said you didn't care about our answer, and that you didn't need anything, so . . . I guess you'll just have to wait and find out when you turn sixteen." Mr. Wakefield grinned.

"*Sixteen?*" Jessica repeated. "I'll die of suspense by then!"

Mrs. Wakefield raised an eyebrow. "We thought you—"

"I know, I know," Jessica broke in. "I don't care about dumb stuff like that." And deep down, she really didn't care.

Not *much*, anyway.

Brian was lying on his cot Sunday afternoon, staring at the ceiling and mindlessly leafing through a sports magazine. He hated being at the Child Protection Center safe house. It might have been safe, but it was boring. There was this cold, impersonal feeling, because everyone who was there didn't want to be and new people came and went all the time.

I wonder what my new family will be like, Brian thought. He'd never wanted to live in Big Mesa, but it was starting to sound good—at least he'd get out of this place.

"Brian Boyd! Phone call!"

Brian sighed and rolled over on his bed. The only phone calls he ever got lately were from his social worker or the guidance counselor at school— his ex-school, now. "How are you doing?" was the first thing they asked. *Rotten—and you?* he always wanted to reply.

"Brian! Come on, he's waiting!" the woman at the front desk yelled down the hall.

Brian stood up and sauntered down the hall to the main office. "Did you say 'he'?"

The desk clerk nodded. "It's a man."

A man? Oh, no—it's my father, Brian thought,

feeling a surge of panic. He knew his father wasn't allowed to contact him till the board made its final ruling, but he couldn't help being nervous anyway. What could he say to his father? What was there to talk about? He picked up the phone. "Hello?" he said cautiously.

"Brian! I'm glad I caught you!"

Brian heaved a sigh of relief. "Mr. Clark?" he asked. Then he started worrying all over again. What was Mr. Clark doing, calling him now? Did he have some other really bad news that he couldn't keep to himself?

"Yes, it's me," Mr. Clark said. "I realize that our last conversation may have been upsetting for you, and I apologize."

"Oh," Brian said, relaxing a little. He tapped the rolled-up magazine against the wall. "Is that it?"

"No, actually, it's not." Mr. Clark cleared his throat. "As I mentioned when we spoke last time, the state decided to send you to another school district, and people here were divided over whether that was a good idea or not. Some wanted you to stay, others thought it might be a good idea for you to . . . move on."

Move away, you mean. "Uh-huh," Brian mumbled.

"Well, I'm happy to report that they've all changed their minds," Mr. Clark said, "thanks to a few students in your English class who got together in support of you. They convinced everyone to sign the petition to keep you in Sweet

Valley. All the parents, all your classmates, all your teachers."

"They *did*?" Brian asked, astonished.

"Yes, they did," Mr. Clark said gently. "We all did."

"But—I don't get it," Brian said, his voice catching in his throat. "I mean, why? You all—" *You all can't stand me*, he added to himself, unable to say the words out loud.

"We all care about you," Mr. Clark told him. "And that's why I asked your social worker to find a family for you right here in Sweet Valley. Of course, the petition we've submitted to the state will have to be read and approved first, but I think it'll go through just fine."

"Oh." For a moment, Brian was too shocked to speak.

They want me to stay in Sweet Valley, he thought. *They don't want me to move away.* All at once he imagined himself hanging out with the guys at Casey's or the video arcade. He imagined people talking to him because they liked him—not just because they felt sorry for him or were afraid of him. For the first time in a long while, he imagined himself fitting in.

Then his excitement vanished. "But Mr. Clark . . . even if this petition works," Brian said, "nobody wants a twelve-year-old with a bunch of problems."

"You're wrong, Brian. We've already found a family for you. And as soon as the petition's all approved, you can move in," Mr. Clark said. "And I'll expect you back in school tomorrow."

"Wow!" Brian said, feeling excited for the first time in weeks. "So . . . wait a second, Mr. Clark. Are you sure it's OK for me to come back to school tomorrow?"

"If you're even one minute late, I'll know," Mr. Clark warned.

Brian laughed. "Yeah—you've got that video camera set up in your office, right?"

"Which reminds me—you and I need to work together to see that you don't spend so much time in my office," Mr. Clark said. "We're willing to give you a fresh start, Brian, but you need to be just as willing to make one."

"Oh, I am," Brian said. "Believe me!" He grinned and leaned against the wall. So maybe everything wasn't a total disaster. He missed his parents, but at least he had a school to go to and people who cared about him.

Maybe later he could call Ken and Todd, tell them the news and see what they were up to. He felt nervous, but excited, too. "So, Mr. Clark. What's the name of this family and when do you think they can pick me up? Is the house nice? Do you think they're going to be good cooks? Because the food here is totally lame. Like, inedible."

Mr. Clark laughed. "Now that sounds more like the Brian I know."

"Lila, I'm telling you, that shirt is *not* going to go on sale—you might as well just buy it now,"

Elizabeth heard Jessica saying as she walked past her on the patio. "And while you're at it—maybe you could buy me one."

"Yeah. Right," Lila replied. "And maybe I'll start buying my clothes off the rack, too." Everyone started laughing like it was the funniest thing they'd ever heard.

Elizabeth smiled at Jessica as she went past. She was glad she and her sister had made up so quickly the week before. She hated it when they weren't speaking.

In the kitchen, Mrs. Wakefield was tossing a giant green salad. "I hope everyone's having a good time," she said as Elizabeth opened the refrigerator. "This is the most last-minute party I've ever tried to put together! Not that I'm complaining about your great idea, Elizabeth."

"I think everyone needed a party," Elizabeth said.

"Thank goodness we have a reason to celebrate," her mother said.

"Right," Elizabeth said. She wrapped her arm around her mother's waist and squeezed tightly. "I'd better get this back outside—Amy and Maria just finished their volleyball game and they're dying of thirst. Thanks for everything, Mom!"

She went out the patio door and into the yard just in time to see the Hublers arrive. Mr. and Mrs. Hubler were two of the nicest people in the whole neighborhood; they had two young children of their own, who at the moment were running around the yard, playing with the Wakefields' croquet set. Brian walked beside Mr. Hubler, his hands in his pockets.

"Hey," Elizabeth said as she walked over to them. "Glad you could make it."

"Thanks for inviting us!" Mr. Hubler said.

"No problem," Elizabeth replied. She turned to Brian. "Help yourself to whatever you'd like to eat and drink."

He nodded and gave her a small smile. "Thanks."

"Sure," Elizabeth said with a shrug.

Just then a Frisbee came sailing right over her head, and she ducked. Brian reached up and caught the Frisbee easily.

"Nice throw, Steven!" Elizabeth yelled.

Steven waved to her. "Come on—you want to play Frisbee?" he called to Brian. "My dad's too busy burning the burgers to play anymore."

"OK," Brian said, casually tossing the disk back to Steven. "But make sure he doesn't burn all of them!"

Steven threw the Frisbee at Brian. "Don't worry, dude. I'll tell him to save two!"

"Hey, better make that four," Brian said, laughing. "I'm starving!"

Elizabeth smiled. She hadn't heard Brian laugh like that since the first time she met him. So everything was working out—or starting to, anyway. He would get a fresh start, thanks to the Hublers.

Now, about those burning hamburgers . . . She ran over to the gas grill, where her father was using a plate to fan the smoke out of his eyes. "It's a good thing Jessica didn't grade you on your barbecue skills," she joked.

"She will," Mr. Wakefield sighed. "One day, I'm sure she will."

"Well, we *could* use a bigger grill," Elizabeth said. "Over at Lila's house—"

"The grill is as big as the pool," her father said, laughing. "Yeah, yeah. I know."

"Hey, Elizabeth. I just wanted to say thanks," Brian said later that evening. He walked over to the table on the Wakefields' patio, where Elizabeth was sitting with Maria.

"OK. Well, thanks for coming," Elizabeth said.

"Sure." Brian shrugged.

Maria stood up. "You know, I should get going, too. You're staying at the Hublers, right?"

Brian nodded. He looked a little embarrassed.

"Cool. I live right around the corner from them. Maybe we could walk together," Maria said.

"Yeah, well . . ." Brian shoved his hands into his pockets. "OK."

"I'll come along, too," Elizabeth offered. "If you guys don't mind. I need the exercise. I think I ate too much."

"Yeah, me too," Brian said as the three of them walked around the house to the front yard. "I probably should have stuck to the *one* burned burger."

Maria laughed. "You think that's bad? I had more ashes than hot dog." She made a face. "It was like chewing a campfire log."

Brian and Elizabeth burst out laughing. "OK, so my dad's not the best at barbecuing," Elizabeth said. "Unless you like the food really well-done."

They walked in silence for a few minutes. Elizabeth felt a little awkward. She still didn't know Brian that well. She hoped she and Maria weren't bugging him by tagging along.

"So, I wanted to thank you," Brian said abruptly when they stopped in front of the Hublers' house. "For the stuff you did. You know, to get me allowed to stay in Sweet Valley."

"Oh," Elizabeth said, surprised. "Well, I didn't do too much."

"Yes, you did," Maria said. "She really did," she told Brian.

He nodded. "I heard. Mr. Bowman and I were talking yesterday. He told me about what happened at the parents' reception."

Elizabeth smiled at him. "Everyone pitched in."

"Yeah," Maria said.

"So," Elizabeth said, putting her hand on the fence around the Hublers' yard. "How do you like living here?"

"It's OK." Brian nodded. "I mean, I'm not really used to it yet. But the Hublers are great. I guess I got lucky."

Elizabeth looked at Brian and smiled. *It's about*

time you had some luck, she thought. *In fact, I can't think of anybody who deserves it more.*

Fifteen minutes later, Elizabeth walked back down the street to her house. It seemed as though everyone had left the party; the only person she could see was Steven. He was running around the driveway, taking shots at the basketball hoop their father had recently put up over the garage.

"Swish!" he yelled as he sank a shot from the lawn. "And the young freshman gives the lead to Sweet Valley!"

"Nice shot," Elizabeth said when she approached.

Steven turned around. "Oh, hey, Elizabeth. Pretty cool, huh? That would have been a three-pointer."

"Really? And where exactly is the three-point line?" Elizabeth teased.

"It's the sidewalk, didn't you know?" Steven said. He grabbed the ball and ran up to the hoop, dunking it. "It was nice of Dad to put this hoop up so short. I bet even you could dunk."

"I don't know about that," Elizabeth said, walking over. "But give me the ball, I'll try a shot anyway." Steven tossed the ball to her. Elizabeth aimed and took a shot. The ball swished through the net and dropped to the pavement, bouncing by Steven's feet.

"Nothing but net! All right, Elizabeth!" Steven cheered, throwing the ball back to her.

Elizabeth shrugged. "What can I say?"

"Not bad," Steven said. "Have you guys been playing in gym class or something?"

"No." Elizabeth dribbled the ball, took a few steps back, and launched another shot. This time the ball bounced off the back of the rim before dropping through the basket.

"Four points for the short Wakefield," Steven said, grabbing the ball and doing a layup.

This is fun, Elizabeth thought as Steven rebounded the ball and tossed it to her. *Why haven't I ever played basketball before?*

We hope you enjoyed reading this book. If you would like to receive further information about available titles in the Bantam series, just write to the address below, with your name and address:

KIM PRIOR
Bantam Books
61–63 Uxbridge Road
London W5 5SA

If you live in Australia or New Zealand and would like more information about the series, please write to:

SALLY PORTER
Transworld Publishers (Australia) Pty Ltd
15–25 Helles Avenue
Moorebank
NSW 2170
AUSTRALIA

KIRI MARTIN
Transworld Publishers (NZ) Ltd
3 William Pickering Drive
Albany
Auckland
NEW ZEALAND

All Transworld titles are available by post from:-
Bookservice by Post
PO Box 29
Douglas
Isle of Man
IM99 1BQ

Credit Cards accepted. Please telephone 01624 675137
or fax 01624 670923

Please allow £0.75 per book for post and packing UK.
Overseas customers allow £1.00 per book for post and packing.